Murder in Limestone County
By Robert D. Coleman

This is a work of fiction. Similarities to real people, places, or events are entirely coincidental.

MURDER IN LIMESTONE COUNTY, BOOK TWO

First edition. May 4, 2019.

ISBN: 979-8230285472

Written by Robert D. Coleman.

Chapter 1

Jake Slone woke up early like he did every day. His days as a Navy Seal had trained him to do that. But he had not had a reason to get up early for the last eight months. Not since he had gotten home from that last job in Afghanistan. But he didn't want to think about how badly that job had gone. His life changed that day.

He got up and went into the bathroom. Looking into the mirror, he didn't like what he saw. His dark hair was longer, almost half-covering his ear. His dark mustache needed trimming badly. A week's worth of beard had filled in around the goatee he normally wore. He has also lost weight. He was down to 208# down from his usual 230#. He looked thin on his 6 foot 2-inch frame.

He shaved and trimmed everything. He then jumped in the shower and cleaned up. He got dressed in jeans and a blue t-shirt as he pulled on his boots. He heard his mother call, "Jake, are you up? Coffee is ready."

Walking into the kitchen. He opened the cabinet and got down his cup. It was a blue cup with the words "world's greatest dad" on the side. He smiles as he remembered the father's day his little girl Michelle had given it to him. She was not little anymore. Almost ten years old.

He poured himself a cup and walked down the hall toward the back door leading to the porch. He stopped and peeked into Michelle's room. She was still sleeping and would be for some time if he knew her.

He walked outside onto the porch, put his coffee down on a table, pulled up a chair, and sat down. He then looked over at his mother, who was already drinking her coffee on the porch. "Morning, Mom," he said. She smiled back at him and said. "Good morning. You sleep well?" He looks away from her and says. "No, not really." I didn't think so, she said. I heard you up several times last night. What's bothering you, son?

Well, Mom, he says. I'm meeting with somebody this morning about going back to work. She turned and looked at him with a surprised look on her face. Are you sure you're ready for that? "No," he says. "But I know we need the money." She then takes a sip of her coffee and looks back over at him. "How long will you be gone?" "Leaving the country?" She asks. "No, not this time." "I ask to keep this one as close to home." " So I should be able to get home every few weeks." "That will be good." She said, "Michelle needs you here as much as you can." " I know, Mom." "I will tell her as soon as I know anything for sure."

He sat there and finished his coffee for about 30 minutes. Looking at his watch, he saw it was almost 7 am. He was meeting his contact at 8 am, so he better get a move on. He liked to be early. Walking back into the house, he grabbed his keys and hat and told his Mom he would be back in a little bit. He started toward the door and then turned around and walked back to his room. He pulled open the top drawer. Inside, he saw his 9mm handgun. He took a long look at it. He had not touched it for the eight months he had been home. He picked it up, checked the clip, put it under his belt behind his back, and made sure his shirt covered it.

He then turned and left the room and walked out of the house. Once outside, he got into a white Ford cargo van. He then started the drive into Tulsa, Oklahoma. His family had lived in and around Tulsa all his life. Until eight months ago, he had not been home for several years.

He drove to Jefferson Park on the east side of town. He parked the van, got out, walked to a park table, and sat down where he could see cars entering the park. Not many people were there, and that was a good thing.

He saw a black car drive into the park, past him, and stop. A man got out, put some sunglasses on, and looked over at him. He walked toward a secluded part of the park and sat down on a park bench. Slone got up and walked toward him. He sat down on the other end of the bench. The man was not anybody that he knew. That kind of bothered him. He reached behind him and felt for the butt of his gun so that he could get to it quickly if he had to.

About that time, the man looks over at him and says. "You must be Slone?" Slone slowly turns his head and says. "Who wants to know?" "That's not important." He said. "I have something for you." He reaches inside his briefcase, pulls out a large envelope and a cell phone, and hands it to Slone. The man then stands up. He looks over at Slone and says. "If you're interested, call the number inside. If not, return all contents to the address inside." The man then turns and walks off.

Slone then watched the man drive off, got up, and walked back to the table next to the van. He sat down and looked at the envelope. He pulled out his knife and broke the seal on it. Inside, he pulled out several pieces of paper. The top page was a list of names and addresses of 14 people. The other pages were pictures and info on all 14 people. All of the people lived in and around Groesbeck, Texas, in Limestone County. There was a smaller envelope inside. When he opened it up, he found 2,000 dollars in 100 dollar bills and a note. The note said: $2,000 dollars advance money, $30,000 each. Slone put the money in his pocket and the pages back into the envelope.

He then took out the phone the man had given him. One number was programmed into the phone. He looked at the phone for a long time and then looked away. This was a huge job. He really didn't want to do it, but he desperately needed the money. There was no way for him to get the money any other way.

He hit the call button on the phone after several rings. A man answered, "Hello" Slone then paused for a second, then said. "I'm in." The man on the other end said. "Good, proceed to the first target." The phone then went dead.

*

The next morning, Slone got up early at 4:30 am. He had said his goodbye's to his mother and Michelle last night. Michelle had taken it hard. She didn't want him to go. He had told her he wouldn't be gone long this time.

He loaded the cargo van with everything he might need. He pulled out at 5 a.m. and drove the 354 miles to Groesbeck in central Texas, stopping only for gas. It took him a little under 6 hours.

The town was small, with less than 4500 people. He was surprised to find that they had three motels. He drove to the post office and opened a P.O. box. He then drove to the Days Inn on the edge of town and checked in.

He rested for a few hours, then got up and took the envelope from his briefcase. He spread the names and pictures on the table. The first name on the list was James Johnson. He was 55 years old, 6 feet tall, and had gray hair. He lived several miles outside of town.

Later that afternoon, he drove out and found the man's house. It was a house sitting way back off the road. Woods surrounded the house. He could watch without being seen.

Slone then turned the van around and headed back into town. He would get started in the morning. This was a big job, the biggest one he had ever taken. But the pay was good, and he needed the money.

*

The following day, he got up early. He wanted to be hidden at the man's house before daylight. He drove out there and found a place to hide the van. He then walked about a mile to the house and sat and watched.

He saw a woman who must have been Johnson's wife leave the house at 7:15 am. Johnson then left the house at 7:45 am. The info he had been given said that they lived there alone, so he felt the house was empty and would be for a while. He walked up to the front door and picked the lock. He wanted a look inside to get the layout of the house.

He walked around for a few minutes and then went back to the door and locked it. He then walked back to the van.

He would watch a few more days. But he was sure he would make the hit at the house.

*

Two days later, after watching Johnson's wife leave at 7:12, he made his move. He quickly made his way to the house and took out his 9mm pistol. He took the silencer out of his pocket and screwed it on the end of his gun. He then walked up to the front door and tried the lock. It was open. He slowly opened the door and went inside. He held his gun low with both hands as he walked down a dark hallway. He saw the light coming from the bedroom. He pulled his gun up high as he entered the bedroom, quickly looking to the left then the right.

He could hear water running in a shower in the connected bathroom. He then entered the bathroom. He could see the man's shadow through the glass of the shower door. Slone opened the shower door. Johnson turned to look at him. Slone shot him in the forehead right between the eyes. Johnson fell back in the shower stall and slowly slid to the floor, dead.

Slone then reached into the shower and turned off the water. Slone takes a towel and lays it over the man's nude body.

Slone went back into the bedroom and looked around, and found the man's wallet. He looked in it and found 147 dollars and took it out. He dropped the wallet on the floor so it would be found. The man had a gold watch on his dresser. He picked it up. He put the money and the watch in the back of the man's dresser, so his wife could find it someday. He was not a thief. But he wanted it to look like a robbery.

As he was leaving, he smelled food in the kitchen. The wife had left Johnson breakfast. Some scrambled eggs and bacon. Slone hated to let food go to waste. So he sat down and ate. After finishing, he put the dishes in the dishwasher. He was careful to wash the fork off with soap and hot water before putting it in, making sure he left no DNA behind. He then left, locked the front door on his way out, and walked back to the van.

Back in the van, Slone took his gloves off, took out the cell phone, and called the number. A man answered. Slone then said. "target #1 has been taken care of." "good," The man said. Do you want to continue? Slone said, "yes." The man said. Look in the mail for payment and move on to #2. Slone said ok and hung up the phone.

The first hit was too easy. He would take some time off before starting the 2nd hit. He would watch the reaction around town and how the police handled it.

Chapter 2

Limestone County Sheriff John Carter heard his alarm go off but didn't move. Pulling the covers up over his head, he heard "John" from a distant voice. He pulled the covers down and opened one eye. "You need to get up," his wife Carolyn said. "But it's Sunday," he said. "No, John, it's Monday," she said as she turned and walked into the bathroom. "Are you sure?" he asked. I think I need a do-over.

He then sat up on the side of the bed and thought to himself. "I hate Mondays!" He got up and slowly walked to the restroom. Carolyn was coming out as he got to the door. He gave her a sleepy look. She kissed him on the cheek and said, "Breakfast will be ready in a few minutes."

He looked in the mirror and said to himself, "Okay, let's get this done." He brushes his teeth and takes a quick shower. He quickly gets dressed in some starched jeans and puts his boots on. He reaches into the closet and pulls out his white shirt. On one sleeve, it says Limestone County Sheriff's Department, an American flag on the other. He tucks his shirttail in and turns and walks over to the dresser, picks up his badge and puts it on the left side of his shirt. He looks in the mirror to make sure everything looks right, then walks back out into the bedroom, grabs his gun belt, and puts it on. He walks over to the gun safe, hits a 6-digit code, opens it up, takes out his 38 pistol, and puts it in his holster.

Walking into the kitchen, he sees Carolyn putting a plate down in front of his chair. He sits down. He looks over at her and says. "Thank you." About that time his son Tom comes and sits down to his left. "Morning, Tom," he says, and the 14-year-old boy settles down. "Hey, Dad," Tom says as he starts eating his breakfast.

Carter then feels arms come around his neck and feels a kiss on the cheek from behind. "Morning, Daddy," Becky, his 14-year-old daughter and Tom's twin, says. Carter smiles and says. "Morning, Sweetheart." She sits down in the chair to Carter's right.

"Daddy," she says. "Don't forget. I'm in the one-act play at the high school tonight at 7:30 pm. You have to be there! I'm the only freshman with a speaking part." He looks at her and smiles. " Yes, I'm so proud of you. I will be there."

Carolyn then comes walking through and says, "I have to go. I'm going to be late." She looks over at John and says. "Can you drop the kids off at school?"

"Sure," Carter says. Becky looks up at her mother and says. "Oh my god, no! Mom. Please take me." "I can't today," Carolyn says as she turns and walks toward the door. Tom smiles big and says, "Yes! squad car!"

Carter gets up from the table and takes his plate to the kitchen sink. He comes back, looks at the kids, and says, "Let's go." Tom jumps up and runs toward the door. Becky looks up at her Dad and says, "My life is over." It will be okay, Carter says. Come on, let's go. She gets up and heads toward the door. Carter walks right behind her, grabs his white straw cowboy hat, and locks the door.

As they get to the car, Becky gets in the front and Tom is standing outside the back of the squad car. "Dad," he says. Carter looks over at Tom. Tom continues, "Can you put the cuffs on me?" "No. Get in," Carter says. Tom gets in the back, Carter starts the car, and they make the short drive to the high school.

About a block away from the school. Becky looks over at her Dad and says. "Please, Dad. Pullover and let me out here." Carter rolls his eyes and pulls the car over. She looks over him, smiles, and says. "Thank you, Daddy. Don't forget the play tonight." "I won't." He says as she leans over and kisses him on the cheek. She gets out, and Carter looks back at Tom. "You getting out here?" "No, Dad he says. Take me up to the front door." Carter then pulls into the school and up to the front door. He stops and gets out. The back door can only be opened from the outside. He opens the door for Tom to get out. Tom looks up at him and says. "Grab me and pull me out, Dad." "Tom just gets out," Carter says. Tom gets out and he closes the door. Tom then puts both his hands on the top of the car. "Pat me down, Dad. Chicks love bad boys! Help a guy out." "Well, first," Carter said. "I would pat you down before I put you in the car. Not after I take you out." Tom then looks up at his Dad and says. "They don't know that." Looking up at the girls at the top of the steps. Carter smiles and says. "Get to class, son." Tom then turns and walks toward the steps and looks over at the girls, who are smiling back at him. Carter shakes his head, smiles, and gets back into the car.

He then drives across town to his Limestone County Sheriff Department office. He had been sheriff for 7 years now. He loved his job. He was up for re-election in a few months. That part of the job he didn't like. He hated everything about the election process. But he had been told by people that should know that he should have no problem getting re-elected. He would be glad when it was over and things got back to normal. He pulled into the parking lot and parked in his spot that said sheriff on it. He wondered why it just said Sheriff and not his name. Maybe the person painting was not that sure he would be re-elected.

Walking inside, he saw several of his deputies walking around and sitting at their desks. They always seemed to start working harder when he walked into the room. He spoke and said good morning to several people as he walked toward his office. He stopped first at his secretary, Nancy Hall's desk. She looked up at him and smiled. "Good morning, Sheriff." "Morning, Nancy," he said as he poured himself a cup of coffee. "You have a guest waiting for you in your office," she said. Carter turned around and looked at her and said. "Who is in my office?" Nancy smiled back at Carter and said, "It's Miss Wilcox." Carter got a surprised look on his face and said. "Miss Wilcox! I can't talk to her now! I don't even have one cup of your god awful coffee in me yet!" "I'm sorry, Sheriff," a smiling Nancy said. "Well, please tell me you at least got some of this bad coffee in her?" "Nope, sorry," she says.

Carter turns and walks toward his office. Several deputies look at him and smile as he walks up, opens the door, and enters.

Carter smiles down at Ms. Wilcox as he walks around behind his desk. "Good Morning, Ms. Wilcox. I'm so sorry to keep you waiting. Can I get you anything, Coffee?" Carter says as he sits down. She looks up at him and says. "No, thank you, sheriff. I'm fine." Carter then smiles and says. "Ok then. What can I do for you?" She looks at him with a stern look on her face. "Well, sheriff, I have a problem with my neighbor. Mr. Bo Brody. I think you know him?" "Yes, ma'am," Carter says. "I know him." "It's those blasted dogs of his!" She says. "He lets them run wild! They come down to my house and dig in my flower bed. And then they lay down when I tried to run them off. That one, he calls Daisy. She assaulted me!" Carter then looked up and said. "The dog bite you?" "No," she said. It was far, far worse. "What did she do?" Carter asks. Ms. Wilcox looks away and then back at him and says. "She licked my feet! And would not stop. Now, every time I come out of the house, she starts licking my feet! Sheriff Something has to be done! I want that man arrested. "ok" Carter said. "Why don't I have one of my deputies drive out there and talk to Mr. Brody? I'm sure we can work something out." "I don't think so, sheriff. This man needs to know you mean business. I demand you take action yourself!" "ok," Carter says as he gets up and walks around the desk. "I will get right on that if you will just give Nancy your number out there. I will get back to you after I talk to him." Ms. Wilcox then got up and walked toward the door. "OK, Sheriff, I will be waiting for your call." "Thank you, Ms. Wilcox," Carter says as she walks out of his office.

Carter closed the door behind her, walked back to his desk, and sat down. He leaned back in his chair. "I guess I will be taking a trip out to the Brody place today," he said, taking a sip of his coffee. He looked at it and frowned. Well, at least it would give him an excuse to get a decent cup of coffee somewhere.

*

(an hour later)

Carter picked up the phone and hit the intercom button. "Billy, can you come in here, please?" A few moments later, Deputy Billy Hayes walked into his office. 'What's up, sheriff?" Hayes said. Carter looked up at Hayes and said. "I'm going to run out to the Brody place. I won't belong. Can you hold down the fort?" "Sure," Hayes says. "Not much going on here this morning." "Ms. Wilcox got problems only you can solve?" Carter walks around his desk and says. "Yes, something like that."

Nancy then walks in with a coffee pot in her hand. "This pot is almost empty. Don't want to waste it." She then pours more coffee in Carter's and Hayes cups. "Thank you." They both say as she walks back out the door. They both look at each other, walk over to the corner of the office, and pour their coffee on the small potted tree in the corner. Carter then looks at Hayes and says. "What does she put in this hair dye?" Hayes laughs and says. "I don't know, but it's bad."

Carter walks out of the office to his patrol car and leaves. He stops at a local gas station and get a cup of coffee and then drives out to the Brody place.

The house is back off the road with a big front porch and a large barn off to the side of the house. As he pulls up in the driveway, he can see several barking dogs. Some were on chains around the barn, and some were running loose. When he gets out of his car, he can see. Bo Brody comes out of the front door. He is a large man. Standing 6 foot 2 or so and heavy, weighing close to 300 pounds, a long scraggly beard and wearing coveralls with a strap over one shoulder.

"Howdy, sheriff," Brody said as Carter walked up to him and shook hands with him. "How are you doing, Bo?" Carter asks. Brody leans over the front porch and spits a stream of tobacco juice. Then says, "Well, I'm doing good. Wish we could get some rain. Maybe cool things off a little bit. Can I get you anything, sheriff?" Brody then turned and shouted inside the house. "Bring the sheriff a beer!" A woman then opens the door and tries to hand Carter a beer. "Oh no. Thank you. I'm fine." She then handed the beer to Brody. "Well, sheriff, no sense letting it go to waste." He says. He twists off the top of the long-neck bottle and takes a long drink. "So, sheriff." He said. "What brings you out here?"

"Well, Bo," Carter says. "I got a complaint about the dogs. They are digging and barking in your neighbor's yard." Brody looks down at Carter and says. "The dogs? It must be that old bitty Wilcox. She just hates Daisy." "Well," Carter said. "She says Daisy assaulted her. By licking her feet." Brody frowns at Carter. "Licking her feet!" he said. "Sheriff, did you ever think maybe that she has dirty feet?" "I'm sure Daisy was just trying to help her out! Well, I have had many a day where I get home and sit down on the porch and take my shoes and socks off. Well, Daisy goes right to work cleaning my feet right up." " With that long tongue of hers. It really feels kind of good sheriff." If the old bitty would just sit back and enjoy it. Or just keep her feet clean. That's the real problem here, Sheriff. She just has dirty feet!"

Carter takes a long look at Brody. Not really knowing what to say to that. "Well, Bo," Carter says. "I think what we need to do. Is just keep the dogs at home. I think that will solve all our problems. You think you can do that for me, Bo?" Brody then nods his head and says. "Sure thing, sheriff. I will try my best." "That's great," Carter says. "I won't take up any more of your time." Brody smiles and says. "Sure you don't want that beer, sheriff? Maybe one for the road?" Carter looks back at him and says. "No thanks."

Carter then gets into his car. He smiles and shakes his head. Did he really just offer the Sheriff of Limestone County a beer to drink on his way back to town?

Chapter 3

Sheriff John Carter sat at his desk, finishing up some paperwork. It was just after 2 p.m. He was trying his best to wrap things up and get out of here on time today. Becky's one-act play at her school was tonight, and he didn't want to miss it.

At about that time, Deputy Greg Roberts walks in. Roberts, Carter, and Deputy Hayes have worked together for a long time. First, they were jailers working their way up, then became Deputies together. When Carter was elected Sheriff, Roberts took the job of Chief Deputy.

Carter looked up at Roberts, who had a serious look on his face. "Don't tell me anything that's going to keep me here past 5 pm," Carter said. "Sorry," Roberts said. "District Attorney James Johnson has been killed." "Killed," Carter said. "Car wreck?" Roberts shook his head. "murdered." He said. "Holy shit!" Carter said. "Where at?" "His house," Roberts said. "Wife went home looking for him after he didn't show for work today. She found him dead. That's all we know now. Hayes was on patrol in the area. He is on his way over there, along with an EMT unit.

Carter then gets up, walks around his desk, and grabs his hat. He looks at Roberts and says, "Let's get over there." They both turn and walk out of the office.

*

(20 minutes later)
Carter and Roberts arrived at Johnson's home. There were already two Sheriff's Department cars there.

When they got to the door, 2 Deputy's were waiting for them. "Where is the wife?" Carter asks. "She is in the other room with

13

Deputy Hayes." One of the young Deputies said. "Ok," Carter said. Turning to the Deputy. "I need you to stay at this door. Nobody but one of us gets in here." He then turns to the other Deputy. "I need you to go in there and keep an eye on the wife. Ask Hayes to come out here with us.

The Deputy turned and walked into the other room, and a moment later, Deputy Hayes came out. Carter, Roberts, and Hayes walked into the bedroom. Carter then turns to Hayes. "Ok, what do you know?" Hayes turns and faces Carter and Roberts and says. "When I got here. I found Ms. Johnson outside waiting for me. She told me that her husband's office had called her when he didn't answer his phone. She said he was in the shower when she left for work this morning. She found his body in the shower. The three men then move into the bathroom and put on gloves. Carter looks inside the shower stall and sees Johnson slumped down on the shower floor with a towel covering his bottom half.

Carter spends several minutes looking at the body, trying to take in every detail. Carter then looks up and asks. "Have we got pictures of this already?" "Yes," Hayes said. "As soon as the other Deputy's got here. I had them take them." "Good," Carter said.

Carter then squats down on one knee. "Looks like he was drying off, and somebody opened the door and shot him in the head. Right between the eyes at close range. Probably with a 9mm." Carter said. Carter then shakes his head, looks up at them, and says, "Something is not right! If he was drying off and was shot. His hands would clench around the towel. They're not. The towel is lying loose over him. Like somebody put it there." Carter then reaches over, picks up the towel and hands it to Roberts. "Bag that," Carter says. Carter then points to a pool of blood on the shower floor. "Look at that. Blood under the towel. Our killer shot him and then covered him with the towel." Roberts looks down at Carter and says. "Why would they do that?"

Carter then stands up and says. "It could be a sign of remorse. Like maybe it was somebody he knew."

They then walk back out of the bedroom. "Hayes then points at the wallet lying on the floor. We found this empty. The wife said she knew he always kept at least 100 dollars in his wallet, but she didn't know for sure how much. She also said his gold watch is gone. If he didn't have it on, he always kept it on the dresser."

"Oh ya, Sheriff. This is where it gets weird." Hayes said. "Wife said she cooked him breakfast. Eggs, bacon, the whole deal and left it on the table for him. She said he was already in the shower when she left." Carter then took a hard look at Hayes and said. "You're telling me. Our killer shot Johnson took what little money he had in his wallet and gold watch. Then sat down and ate the man's breakfast?" "Yes," Hayes said. "That's kind of what it looks like." Roberts then looks over at Carter and says. "Sheriff, what kind of a sick fucker are we dealing with?"

Carter then looked around. "If robbery was the motive. Why didn't he ransack the house and take more than his watch and pocket money?" Carter asks.

They then turned and walked through the house to the kitchen. Carter looked around and said. "Look, he even put his dishes in the dishwasher. I want everything in that dishwasher bagged up. We might get lucky and get some DNA."

"Ok," Carter said. "Let's talk to the wife." The three men walk down a hall to the study area where Johnson's wife has been waiting with a deputy. They walked into the room. Carter looked over at the woman sitting on the sofa. She was tall, thin, had dark red hair, and was at least 20 years younger than Johnson. Carter extended his hand and said. "I'm Sheriff John Carter. I'm very sorry for your loss." Ms. Johnson stood up and takes Carter's hand and says. "Thank you." Carter then looks at her and says. "We need to ask you a few questions. If that is alright?" She looks over at Carter and says. "I have told your deputy all I know." "Yes, ma'am I know Carter said. But we need to go over it again. Just so we know we got it all covered." "Yes, of course." She said. She then turned and sat on a sofa, and Carter pulled up a chair across from her.

"Ok," Carter said. "Do you know of anybody who would want to hurt your husband? She shakes her head. "No. Everybody loved James." "Ok," Carter said. "This morning. Can you walk us through what happened this morning?" "Well," she said. "I got up first, and he got up about 30 minutes after me. I have to be at work at 7:30 am, and he doesn't have to be there till 8:00 am. I got dressed, fixed his breakfast, and left it on the table for him. I went back to the bedroom, and he was in the shower. I said goodbye and left about 7:15 am or so." "And he was still in the shower when you left?" Carter asks. "Yes," she said. "I could hear the water running." Carter then looks away and then back at her and says. "Think real hard. As you were leaving. Did you see anything out of the ordinary? Any little thing might be important?" "No, nothing." "Ok," Carter said. "Then what made you come home and check on him?" She then says. "His office called and said he had not shown up for work or court this morning. And that he was not answering his phone. I then tried to call him several times with no answer. I then drove home and found him in the shower, dead." She then lowers her head down in her hands.

Carter then reaches into his pocket, pulls out a card, and hands it to her. "If you think of anything else. Anything at all. Can you please call me?" "Yes, of course." She said. "Is there any place you can stay for a few days?" Carter asks. She looks up at him and says. "Yes, my sisters." "Good," Carter says. "I will have one of my deputies drive you."

Carter looks over at the deputy who had been waiting with her. "Can you drive Ms. Johnson to her sisters?" "Sure thing, Sheriff." He says. Ms. Johnson then walked out with the deputy.

Carter, Roberts, and Hayes stand there looking at each other for a minute. Carter then says. "As soon as she is gone we need to get the body over to the M.E. office and tell Dr. Graves that we need a rush job on this one. "Hayes then looks over at Carter and says. I will call them to come to get him." Hayes then turns and leaves the room.

Roberts looks over at Carter and says. "So, what you think?" "I don't know," Carter says. "Some things point to the wife. Like almost nothing was taken. And then covering him up. She didn't seem to be all that upset. But then we got the headshot. A woman would not do that. She would shoot for the body. Then we got breakfast eaten by somebody. So my gut feeling is that she didn't do it. But if it was somebody else. You were right. This guy is one sick fucker!"

Carter and Roberts then hear a familiar voice coming down the hall. They look up to see Groesbeck Mayor Bobby Bozeman walk through the door. He is a short, 5ft 9in, heavy bald man with a thick mustache. He is followed by the Deputy who had been at the door. "Sorry, Sheriff, he pushed right by me." The Deputy says. It's okay," Carter says. Just get back on the door."

Mayor Bozeman looked at Carter and said. "Is it true, Sheriff? Is District Attorney Johnson really dead?" Carter then takes a long hard look at Bozeman and says. "Yes, it's true. Now you need to get the hell out of here! You're contaminating my crime scene!" Bozeman got a surprised look on his face and then said. "Well, Sheriff, I need to know what's going on. Do you have any suspects? Do you have any leads? Oh my god! Do you think he is targeting city leaders? Do I need protection? What about the press? What are we going to tell the press?" Carter, with a shocked look on his face, says. "Oh my god! You need to shut the fuck up! We are just getting started, and we are not telling you or the press or anybody else anything! The last thing we need is you out running your mouth!"

Bozeman then cocked his head back and said. "Sheriff. I'm the Mayor of Groesbeck, and I demand answers" Carter then turned red in the face and said. "We are clearly at least 5 miles outside the city limits of Groesbeck. That makes it the jurisdiction of the Limestone County Sheriff's Department. I'm the Sheriff. I don't work for you! Now get the hell out of my crime scene, or I will arrest you for obstruction of justice!" Bozeman then looked at Carter and said. "Ok, Sheriff, if that's the way you want to play it. This is an election year. If you're not careful, you might be out of a job." He then turned and walked out.

Carter then looked over at Roberts, who was trying not to laugh. "What?" Carter said. Roberts smiled and said. " Y'all don't like each other much, do you?" "Not really," Carter said. "We have some history," Roberts smiled and said. "Ya, arresting his son will do that!" Carter then looks around at Roberts. "No, His son being a drug dealer will do that!"

*

(Several hours later)

It was about 7:30 when Carter, Roberts, and Hayes returned to the office. Walking into the squad room followed by several Deputies carrying boxes of stuff. Carter pointed to the conference room and said. "Let's get everything set up in there." Nancy then walks up and hands Carter a cup of coffee. Carter looks at her and says. "Why are you still here, Nancy?" She says. "Because with the 3 of you go to the same call. Somebody has to run this office." She looks over at Roberts and Hayes. "There is plenty of coffee over there." They smiled back at her as she walked away.

Carter then turned to Roberts and said, "What time is it?" Roberts looked at his watch and said, "It's 7:35 p.m." Carter turned and looked at the clock on the wall. Hey, can you handle things here for about an hour?" Carter said. Sure. What's up?" Roberts said. As Carter was heading to the door, Carter turned back around. "I got to go be a Dad!"

*

Carter pulled up outside the High School's auditorium. Stopped his car and jumped out. Becky's play was tonight, and she would be so upset if he missed it. He quickly opened the door and went inside. A woman was sitting at a table and had been taking money. She looks up at him and says. "The play has already started." "That's ok." He says as he puts money on the table. He then walks toward the door. She shouts back at him. "You have change coming!" "Keep it." He says.

He opens the door, and it is dark inside. He will never find Carolyn in the dark. He turns and walks back outside and down the hall to the back of the stage. He opens the door and walks in. He walks up to the side of the stage where he can see the actors on the stage. He finds Becky. He smiles. He then hears a voice from behind him. "Hey, Dad, what you doing back here?" Carter turns to find his son Tom. "Hey, I was late, so I came back here." Tom then looks up at his Dad and says. "You're really not supposed to be back here." Carter looks over at his son. "So go find a cop. Has she said her line yet?" "No, not yet. It's fixing to come up." Tom says. They both turn to look at the stage. They see Becky step toward the audience and point and say. " There. I see a ship!" Tom then rolls his eyes and says. "I think I see an Oscar in this for her!" Carter frowns and looks at Tom. "You get Tony's for plays. Not Oscar's." Tom turns with a surprised look on his face. "Oh, my bad."

The curtain closed, and Becky comes off stage and sees Carter. "Daddy, you made it." She runs over and hugs her Dad. Carter smiles big and says. "You were great." "Thanks, Daddy," she says. Carter then turns and looks at both kids. "Look, guys, I got to go. I have a lot going on at work. I'm sorry." "Thanks for coming, Daddy," Becky says. Tom looks up at his dad. "What's going on at work to keep you this late?" "I can't get into it now, Tom. I will try to get home before you go to bed. Tell Mom I will be home in a little while."

Carter turns and leaves. He wishes he was going home with them and not back to the mess he had at the office. This morning, his biggest problem was a foot-licking dog. Now, he had a dead District Attorney.

He had a feeling that he was going to have a lot of long days and late nights for a while.

Chapter 4

Jake Slone was up early. Like he was every day. It had been a week since the first hit. He felt it had gone well. A few days ago, his money came in the mail. 28,000 dollars in hundred dollar bills. He had not gone out much. Just going out to eat and get a newspaper. From what he had read and heard on TV about the murder. They said Johnson was killed in his home. In an apparent robbery.

He had packed his stuff up. He was moving to a new hotel today. He didn't like to stay in one place for too long. He put his bag over his shoulder, picked up his suitcase, and stepped outside in the hallway. He looked down the hall and saw the cleaning lady. She had been very nice to him. Getting him towels and anything else he had to ask for. He put his bags down and walked down to the end of the hall where she was at. He looked over to her and smiled, and said. "I'm checking out today. You have been very helpful. Thank you." He then reached in his pocket and handed her a 100 dollar bill. She has a very surprised look on her face. "Oh my. Thank you, sir, thank you so much!" Slone then smiles, turns, walks back to his bags, and picks them up. He knew she worked very hard and could use the extra money. He then walked down to the lobby and checked out.

Slone then drove to the local cafe to get an early lunch. The waitress walked him to his table and gave him his menu. Sitting down, he looked out the window. Groesbeck was a nice little town. Everybody knew everybody. So there was a lot of talk around town about the Johnson murder. But nobody knew much. A robbery was the only motive that anybody talked about. But Slone knew that the Sheriff Department had dismissed the robbery motive quickly.

Slone ate his lunch and drove across town to another motel. He got checked in and got settled into his room. After he had unpacked, he sat down at the table and took out the list of names. The first name Johnson had been marked off. The next name on the list was a man named Sam Logan. Logan was a farmer who lived alone several miles outside of town. He was a middle-aged man with gray hair.

Later that afternoon Slone got in the van and drove out to the Logan place. He found a place to hide the van, and then he walked up to the house and found a place he could hide and watch. About 6 pm that afternoon. Logan came out and walked down to the barn. He fed and watered the calves in the pen and then got in his truck, drove off in the pasture, and gave the cows some hay and range cubes. Slone saw an open water well behind the bard that he used to water the animals. After Logan went inside Slone walked down to the barn and looked around. He probably did the same thing every day. He had his plan now. Slone then drove back to the motel and got a good night's rest.

*

(Next day, 4:30 pm)

Slone sat on the bed watching TV. He looked at his watch and saw it was time. He got up and put on a black pair of pants and a black shirt. He then left the room and walked down to the parking lot. He got into the van, drove to the Logan place, and hid the van. He moved to the back of the van. He got his 9mm gun and put it in the holster under his left arm. He picked up the silencer and put it in his pocket. He then grabbed a black net cap that would pull down over his face. He got out of the van and made the ½ mile walk to the barn. Inside, he hid in the back where he could see the door. He took out the silencer, put it on the 9mm, and waited.

At approximately 6:00 pm, Logan came out and went to the barn to care for the animals. He didn't see Slone hiding behind some hay. Slone waited for the right time when Logan had his back to him. Slone pointed the gun and aimed it at Logan's head. He fired a single shot that hit Logan in the back of the head. He then fell to his knees and then face down dead.

Slone then took out a small plastic trash bag and put it around Logan's head and put a large rubber band around his neck to keep from getting blood all over everything. He then lifted the body over his shoulder and walked out behind the barn to the well and dropped the body in. Slone then returned to the barn and cleaned up the little amount of blood that had gotten onto the dirt floor.

Slone then let the calves in the pen out to pasture so they could get grass and water. It might be weeks before Logan was missed, and he didn't like to abuse animals.

He then slowly walked back to the van, took out his cell phone, and made the call. When the man answered, Slone simply said, "Number 2 has been taken care of." The man on the other end just said, "Look for payment and continue." The phone went dead, and Slone put it away, started the van, and drove into town. He picked up a hamburger and fries, drove back to the motel, and ate.

The first two had been very easy. From here on out, it would get harder. Much harder.

*

(3 days later)

Sheriff John Carter sat at his desk and looked at the report on the Johnson murder. Robbery- who would drive all the way out there to rob somebody and then kill them? It had to be somebody that Johnson knew. Maybe somebody that Johnson had sent to prison? But no one he had prosecuted had gotten out in the last few months. Johnson also had a reputation around town of being a womanizer. If he had another woman on the side he had kept her hidden well. He knew he had some problems with his wife. Maybe she knew he had another woman and killed him. Some things point to that but his gut feeling was that she didn't do it. But right now, she was his only suspect. If he had another woman on the side he had to find her. She would be a suspect too, and maybe she had a husband or a boyfriend. But right now, there were too many questions and not enough answers.

Carter then heard a knock on his door. Carter looked up and said. "Come in." Billy Hayes walked in and said. "I just took a missing person report on Sam Logan. You know him, don't you?" "Yes," Carter said. "I have known him for a long time." Hayes sat down and said. "His son Sam Jr. Had called and said that his father had not been home in three days and didn't say he was leaving town, and his car is still at the house. I was just heading out to the Logan place. You want to come?" Carter looked at him and said. "Bring the car around and meet me in front."

Hayes pulled the car around, Carter got in, and they left for the Logan place. It was about 15 miles outside of town.

Carter had known the Logan family for a long time. He had gone to school with Sam Jr., and his father had lived alone since his mother died a few years ago.

They pulled up to the house and got out and walked up to the door and knocked. Sam opened the door, looked at Carter, and smiled. "Hey John, Thanks for coming," he said. Extending his hand to shake. Carter took Sam's hand and said. "Sure thing, Sam." Carter turned to Hayes and said. "This is Deputy Hayes." Hayes and Sam then shook hands, and Sam said. "Come in." They followed Sam to the living room. Sam sat down in a chair at the end of the coffee table, and Carter and Hayes sat down on the sofa to the side.

"Ok," Carter said, "When is the last time you heard from your father?" Sam looks over at Carter and says. "It's been about 3 days. We talk almost every day. So when I did not get in touch with him, I drove over here. I get here to find the door unlocked and his car and truck in the driveway. I come in and look around, and it looks like all his stuff is still here. I went upstairs to the bedroom and looked in the medicine cabinet, and his blood pressure medicine was still there. There is no way he would leave without that." Carter then looked over at Sam and said.

Is there any chance he maybe had a 2nd bottle of pills he could have taken with him?" "Not likely," Sam said. "He only bought it a month at a time." Hayes then said. "Have you talked to anybody else that might have talked to him in the last 3 days?" "Well," Sam said. " Dad kept mostly to himself. Just the store on Saturday and church on Sunday. Then, there was taking care of the livestock. That kept him busy."

Carter then stands up and says, "Ok, Sam. Mind if we take a look around?" Sam then stands up and says, "Sure, look all you want. Maybe you will see something that I didn't."

Carter and Hayes then walk around the house and look around. Everything looked in place. Nothing missing that they could see. There were no signs of a beak in. They then walked outside to the barn. Carter looked around. Something didn't look right. There was a large round bale of hay in the pen, with a hay ring around it and the string cut off. There was also water in the water trough. The pen had hoof prints all over it like there had been calves in the pen. But the gate was closed, so nothing could get in here.

Carter then saw the water well and walked out to it. He looked around. Something was not right about this, and Carter had a bad feeling about it.

Chapter 5

Slone got in his van and drove to the Post Office. It had been three days since the Logan hit. He parked the van, got out, and looked around. There was not much going on in town today. He walked up the steps. He stopped and held the door open for the elderly lady walking behind him. She smiled and said, "Thank you." Slone smiled back at her and nodded his head.

Inside, he walked around the corner and found his P.O. Box. He took out his key and opened it. Inside was the envelope he was expecting. He quickly took it out, put it in his coat pocket, and locked the box back. He turned and walked toward the door, passing another younger woman. He smiled at her and said, "Good morning." She smiled back at him as he walked through the doors and back out to the van.

He then drove back to the motel and went up to his room. He took the envelope out and placed it on the table. He then took his coat off and sat down at the table. He opened the envelope, took out the money, and counted it. Thirty thousand dollars was the right amount. He had enough money now to at least get started. He would be glad when this job was done and he could move on.

Slone then took out the list of names and looked at it. The third name on the list was a woman named Pam Smith. She was a 35-year-old married stay-at-home mom of 2 kids who lived in the middle of town. This hit was going to be more difficult. He wondered what a 35-year-old stay-at-home mom had done to get on the list. But he had to put that out of his mind, he had a job to do.

He got up, went down to the van, drove to the address, and looked around. It didn't look like anybody was home. There was an alley behind the house. He walked down the alley and looked around. The alley provided better access to the house. He walked back to the van and returned to the motel and planned the hit for the next day.

The next morning, Slone got up at 5:00 am. I got dressed in all black, got in the van, and drove to Smith's house. No lights were on. So he drove back to a gas station and got gas and something to eat. He then drove back and parked the van in the alley. He got out, opened the back of the van, took out a big magnet sign that said cable TV repair service on it, and placed it on the side of the van. Anybody seeing it would not think it was out of place. He walked about a half a block to the house and waited. At about 6:30 am, her husband left. At about 7:45 am, she came out with two kids and left. He then went into the backyard, picked the lock on the back door, and went inside. He hid in a back bedroom and waited for her to get home.

At about 8:10 am, he heard her open the door. He took a piece of wire out of his pocket. He walked down the hall and heard her in the kitchen. He slowly approached her. Before he got close enough, she turned around and saw him and screamed. He quickly grabbed her, put the wire around her neck, and squeezed very hard. She reached up and scratched his neck, drawing blood. She then went limp, and he let her down to the floor and checked to see if she was dead, and she was.

He picked up the body and took her to the bedroom. He put her on the bed and took her shirt and pants off. He picked up her shirt, tore it, and threw it on the floor. He then poisoned the body on the bed to make it look like she had been raped.

He left by the back door and down the alley to the van and got in. As he started driving away, he felt a burning sensation on his neck. He reached for his neck and looked down at his hand and saw the blood on it. He then said. "Oh shit!" He had left blood at the house. If they had blood, they would have his DNA. That could be a big problem.

*

Sheriff John Carter looked up from his desk to see Deputy Billy Hayes walk in. Hayes looked at him and said. "We got another dead body! A woman this time, her name was Pam Smith. Her kids found her dead. Carter got up and said. "What's going on in this town? Let's go!"

When Carter and Hayes got to the house, the Groesbeck Police were already there. They walked in and found Police Chief Joe Jordan. "Hi, John," Jordan said. "What you got, Joe?" Said Carter. Jordan then turned to the body lying on the bed. "We got a woman, Pam Smith, 35 years old. Strangled with some kind of wire, after she had been raped. But we may have a break. We found blood on the bed and in the kitchen that we think might be the killers. And she has some skin and blood under her fingernails."

Carter put on some latex gloves, picked up her hand, and looked at the fingers and nails. "It looks like there will be enough to get some DNA. If we have him in the system, maybe we can get a match. If not, we can find something to match him to if we catch him.

Carter looks over at Jordan. "I thought this might be connected to the Johnson murder. But looks like the MO is not the same. But you want to work this one together?" Jordon nodded his head. "Sure. I'm not going to turn down help. You have a lot more manpower than I do."

Carter and Hayes walked around the house and looked around. They saw were the few drops of blood that had been found in the kitchen. "Looks like this is where it started," Hayes said. They then turned and walked to the bedroom. The body was lying across the bed. Carter bent down and looked at her neck. "Look at this," Carter said. "She has a clear ring mark around her neck. She was strangled from behind. Using a thin wire or something." Carter then stands up and looks at Hayes. "I think this was staged to look like a rape. I think she was killed in the kitchen." Hayes then looked over at Carter and said. "So you think this might be the same guy?" Carter then took his gloves off and said. "At first, I didn't think so. But now my gut is telling me it is. Well, get the body over to Dr. Graves for an autopsy. I'm betting she wasn't raped."

Carter's phone then rang. "Hello," Carter said, answering his phone. "Okay, get over there. Get the Fire Department to help you if you need to. We will be over there as soon as we are done here." Carter then put his phone away and said, "That was Roberts. Sam Logan Jr. called and said there was a strong smell coming from the well behind the barn.

*

2 hours later

When Carter and Hayes arrived at Logan Place, Deputy Greg Roberts met them at the car. As Carter and Hayes got out, Roberts said, "We went down in the well and found a body. We are fixing to bring it out."

Carter, Hayes, and Roberts then walked down to the well. A man from the Groesbeck Fire Department was pulling what looked like a badly decomposed body out of the well. As Carter got closer, he could see that the body was a man. Most likely, Sam Logan. But the body was too badly decomposed to tell that for sure. The body had a bag around the head. That quickly ruled out that Sam had fallen in the well by accident. When they took the bag off, they could clearly see a gunshot wound.

Carter then looked over at Roberts and Hayes. "Let's get him over to the morgue. So Dr. Graves can get a look at him.

Carter then turns and walks away. Dr. Graves was going to be a very busy man.

Chapter 6

The next morning, Carter sat at his desk, looking over everything they had on the Johnson, Logan, and Smith murders, as he drank the last of his third cup of Nancy's very bad coffee.

He had nothing for sure that the 3 cases were connected. But how could three murders happen this close together in this area? It's not like this is New York or Los Angeles. It was Groesbeck, for God's sake. This does not happen here.

Deputy Hayes stuck his head in the door and said. "Dr. Graves, on line one." "Thanks," Carter said. Reaching for the phone. "This is Sheriff Carter," He said. "Sure thing, Doc, I will be right over." Carter then hung up the phone, got up and walked around his desk, grabbed his hat off the back of the door and walked out of the office. He looked over at Hayes sitting at his desk. "I'm headed over to see Dr. Graves." Hayes looked over at him and said. "Ok, Boss, let me know what you find out."

Carter then walked to his car and made the short drive over to Limestone County Medical Center. The morgue was located at the back of the hospital. You could get in two ways. Going all the way through the hospital or going in through a side door. You could open the side door with a keycard or a 4-digit code. Carter was one of the few people outside of hospital personnel who knew the code. He punched in the code, opened the door, and walked in. Down the hall to the right was Dr. Dan Graves's office. Dr. Graves had been the Limestone County Medical Examiner for well over 20 years. He was short and overweight, with a thick gray beard.

When Carter reached his office, he walked in to find Dr. Graves sitting behind his desk, looking at some papers. He looked up at Carter. "Morning John. How are you doing this morning?" "Well, Doc,"

Carter said. I will be doing a lot better when we catch this guy who keeps sending you so much business." Graves then got up and walked around his desk, saying, "Well, let me show you what I got, and hopefully, you can do that."

They both turn and walk out of the office and across the hall to the autopsy room. Inside the large room were two tables, and on one end, there were cold compartment drawers where the bodies were kept. Graves then walked over, opened a doo,r and pulled out a body. It was covered with a sheet. Graves pulled the sheet back. It was the body of Sam Logan that had been pulled out of the well. Graves said. "Looks like he died from a gunshot wound to the back of the head." Carter then looked over at Graves. "What kind of gun?" Carter asks. "Well, it's the bullet went all the way through the skull and exited. It's hard to tell without the slug." Graves said. "Could it have been a 9mm?" Carter asks. "Yes, very well could be," Graves said. "How long has he been dead?" Carter asks. "Graves looked over at Carter and said. "Probably a week to 10 days."

Graves then closed the drawer and walked down to the next one. "This one told me a lot more," he said. He opened the drawer and pulled out another body. This one was Pam Smith. Graves looked over at Carter and said. "She was strangled with a thin wire. But she put up a fight. I found blood and tissue under her fingernails, enough to get some DNA. I'm going to get that sent off to the lab as soon as I can. Right now, all I know is that it's type O positive blood. She has type A-positive blood. "Well," Carter said. "That leaves about half of Limestone County with O positive blood." "That's probably right. But the guy has a bad cut probably on his neck." Graves said.

Carter then looked over at the doctor and said. Is there anything that can connect the Johnson, Logan, and Smith murders to the same man?" Graves then said. "Johnson and Logan were both shot in the head. Maybe with the same weapon. But we don't know that for sure." "Was Smith Sexually assaulted?" Carter asks." "No," Graves said.

"There was no rape." Graves then closed the drawer. "Ok, Thanks, Doc. That's all I need. As soon as you get that DNA, let me know." "Sure will, and if I turn anything else up, I will give you a call." "Thank you," Carter said as he turned to leave.

Walking out to his car, Carter thought. There was nothing really to link the murders together. But something deep down in his gut told him it was the same man. He knew it. Somehow, he just knew it!

*

Jake Slone sat at the table in his hotel room and looked at his laptop. He had found plans to the Limestone County Medical Center. At one end of the hospital was the morgue. He was sure that's where they had taken Pam Smith. They had probably already done the autopsy on her. He was sure they had found his DNA under her fingernails. It was also likely that they didn't have the equipment they would need to break the blood down. They would have to send it off to a lab. Which meant it would have to go out by a secure carrier. Most likely in the morning.

He had to get it back. It was a risky move, but one he felt he had to take. He needed the money, but it would do him no good if he got caught.

Slone waited several hours for it to start getting dark. He got dressed in all black. He put what tools he might need in a bag and put it over his shoulder. He went out by a side door, not wanting to walk through the lobby. He got in the van and made the short drive to the hospital.

He watched and waited for a little while. It looked like they had one security guard that came around about every hour. He made one last check of his bag for things he might need. He put his gun holster on. He checked his 9mm gun and put it back in the holster. He hoped he would not need it. He got out of the van, put on his gloves, and pulled down a ski mask over his face. He made the quick walk up the dock to the side door. The lock opened with a card swipe or a number code. He had a scanner he could put on the lock just above the number pad, and it would give him the numbers. But that would take a few minutes, and he was out in the open. He looked at the number pad. Looked like three numbers were worn down and dirty from being used a lot. He thought to himself. Surely not. But what did he have to lose? He punched in the numbers 0911. The light on the door flashed green and opened.

Slone then entered and walked down the long hall. He turned and entered the large room where they did the autopsy. On one end were refrigerator drawers where they stored the bodies. There were two tables in the middle. On the other side was a desk and chair, some file cabinets, and a refrigerator with a glass door on it.

He started walking that way toward it when he heard a nose. He quickly pulled out his gun and found a place to hide behind some more file cabinets. At about that time, the door opened, and the security guard came walking in. He didn't look around he just walked straight to the desk and sat down. Slone watched as he took off his shoes and leaned back in the chair, put his feet up on the desk, leaned back, and closed his eyes.

Slone waited a moment, thinking about what to do. He then stood up and slowly and quietly walked over to the man. He stood over him, looking down at him. Slone then said. "Hey, you." The man jumped in his chair and opened his eyes. To see Slone standing over him with a ski mask over his face, pointing a gun at him. The man's hands shot up as he said. "I have a little bit of money in my wallet. It's yours. Just please don't kill me." Slone then looked at the man for a long moment and said. "I don't want your money." The man then looked up at him and said. "Drugs, you want drugs. There is not any in here. But I can help you find some. I know where they keep them. Just please don't kill me!" Slone then turned the man's chair around to face away from him. And said. "I don't want drugs. And I'm not going to kill you." Slone then took some zip ties out of his bag and tied the man's hand behind him around the back of the chair.

Slone then looked through the files that were lying on the desk. He found the one with the name Pam Smith on it. He opened it up and found the case number on it. He then walked over to the glass-cased refrigerator. Inside was an envelope addressed to a lab in Dallas, Texas. He opened it up to find two small samples of blood and tissue with a case number that matched the one on Pam Smith's file. This was it. He put the samples in his pocket.

He then walked back over to the security guard. "Is anybody going to be looking for you?" he asked. "No." The man said. Slone then walked behind the man, reached down, and loosened the ties on the man's hands. He then walked around in front of the man and said. "Ok, here's the deal. I loosened you up. You should be able to work yourself free in about 30 minutes or so. But before you run out of here. Put your shoes back on!" Slone then turned and walked toward the door. He stopped and turned around and faced the man. "Oh, and one more thing. 0911 really! That's insulting! Change that!"

Slone then walked out the door and back to the van. Well, it hadn't gone as well as he had hoped. But he had got what he wanted.

*

Carter was in a deep sleep and didn't hear his cell phone going off on his nightstand. His wife, Carolyn, reached over to him and grabbed his phone. "Hello. Hey Greg. Ya, he is here. Hang on." She said. She then straddled her husband and put her head on his chest, and she said. "John, wake up the phone." Carter raised his head up and said. "What?" She looked up at him and said. "Greg Roberts on the phone." She then handed him the phone. "Hey," he said. "What? Are you kidding me? Ok, I will be right over." He laid his phone back over on his nightstand. He looked up at his wife and said. "I have to go." She picked her head up off his chest and said. "Is somebody Dead, dying, or missing?" "No," he said. She smiled at him. "Then I need 15 more minutes." She then started kissing on his chest and working her way down. "Babe, I really need to go." He said. About that time, she took him all into her mouth. He laid his head back hard into his pillow and said. "Ok, what's 15 minutes!" He then reached down and pulled her up, kissed her, and rolled over on top of her. Pinning her arms up over her head. Her eyes got big, and she smiled as he entered her. He looked down into her eyes and said. "Well, maybe 30." As he reached down and passionately kissed her.

*

(45 minutes later)

Carter pulled into the hospital parking lot down on the morgue end. As he got out and walked toward the door. He saw Deputy Roberts walking toward him. "Hey, boss, what took you so long? You live like a half-mile away." Carter then looked over at Roberts and said. "Traffic was bad. What do we have?" As both men started walking toward the door. Roberts said. "Seriously, traffic? It's Groesbeck at night!" Carter stopped and took a hard look at Roberts. Roberts then smiled. "Well, ok. Looks like someone broke into the morgue and took something. Don't know what or why. We do have a witness. The hospital security guard. Carter then looks at him and says. "Oh, yeah. That's good. What did he have to say?" "Well, " Roberts said. "I will let him tell you."

They then walked inside and saw a few other deputies working and the security guard sitting in a chair. The walked over to him. Roberts said. "This is Sheriff Carter. Tell him what you told me." The guard stood up and shook hands with Carter. "Well, Sheriff, it was like this. I came in through the hospital door, making my regular rounds. Then I heard a noise coming from inside the examination room. I slowly opened the door to see this man going through the samples in the refrigerator. I shined my flashlight on him and told him to stop. He then came at me, I hit him in the mouth with a right and then left.

He falls back on the desk, and that's when he pulls his gun on me. He ties me to the chair and finds what he was looking for, and leaves. You know, if they would let me carry a gun, I could have ended this for you." Carter then says to him. "Did you get a look at his face?" "No." The man said. "He had a mask on." Carter then said. "Ok, we will need you to fill out a statement form and give as much detail as you remember." "Sure thing, Sheriff." The man said.

Carter and Roberts then turn and walk away. What do you think? Roberts asks. "I think if he hit him with a right and then a left, his hands would be at least scuffed up. And if he had a gun. He would have pulled it out before coming at him." Roberts nodded. "That's what I think too. I talked to some of the nurses. They say he comes down here to sleep after he makes his rounds.

Carter and Roberts look around the room. Carter finds a box that has been opened on the table. It's addressed to the lab in Dallas. "Looks like what he wanted was in this box," Carter said.

About that time. Dr. Graves walked in. Carter turned to the doctor and said. "Please, Doc, tell me that the DNA recovered from the Smith murder was not in this box?" Dr. Graves walked over and looked at the box and said. "I'm afraid so, John. It was set to go out first thing in the morning. Roberts then looks at them and says. "So our killer breaks in here and steals back his DNA. So we have nothing on the guy now!

Carter lowers his head and takes a few steps away. He turns back to face Roberts and Graves and says. "Well, we do know one thing now. We are not dealing with a random killer. And we are not dealing with a sicko serial killer." Roberts then looks at Carter and says. "So what are we dealing with, boss?" Carter looks at Dr. Graves and then back at Roberts and says. "We are dealing with a professional. Or in other words. A hitman!

Chapter 7

Slone woke up early as he always did. He got up and fixed him a cup of coffee and sat down at the table in his room.

The 3rd hit had been the most difficult. He felt the bandage on his neck. He had made a huge mistake letting her scratch him and leaving his DNA there. But he had corrected that mistake. Running into that security guard could be a problem. But he had a mask on covering his face. He couldn't worry about that now.

He took out the envelope and looked at the 4th name on the list. It was a man in his 30s. His name was Stanley Cox. He lived in the town of Mexia, about 10 miles from Groesbeck.

Later that afternoon, Slone got in his van, drove to the post office, and picked up the money from the 3rd hit. He then drove to Mexia and found where Cox lived. It was a large house in a nice part of town. A truck was in the front with a bass boat and trailer hooked up. As he watches the house, it looked like he was getting ready for a fishing trip. Tomorrow was Sunday. He was going fishing tomorrow. Slone then left and drove back to the motel.

The next morning, he got up early and drove back to the Cox house. He got there about 4:45 a.m., parked the van, and waited a little way down the street.

At about 5:30 am, Cox came out of the house. He looked over the boat. Checking the tires and then got in the truck, backed out of the driveway, and left. Slone followed him the 10 miles back to Groesbeck and then east to Lake Limestone. He found a place to watch as Cox put the boat in the water. He then got out of the van and started looking for a boat to steal. He found a small boat chained to a dock about a quarter of a mile down the bank. He took a pair of small bolt cutters out of his bag and cut the chain. He got in the boat and rowed out into the lake before starting the motor.

There were not that many boats on the lake this time of the morning. It was just now starting to get light outside. He quickly found a light on a boat that he was sure was Cox. He cut off his motor and started rowing toward Cox. When he got close, he started yelling at Cox. "I need some help! My boat is taking on water fast." Cox heard him and said. "Hang on, I'm coming over." Slone sat down in the boat and put the silencer on his gun. He waited for Cox to get close. Cox handed a line to him, and he tied it to his boat. Cox then looked in the boat and said. "I thought you were taking on water?" Slone looked at him and said. "No, I'm very sorry." He then pulled out his 9mm with the silencer and shot Cox in the head.

Cox then fell to the bottom of his boat. Slone then boarded his boat and started to pick him up when he heard a sound. He then dropped the body back down in the boat when he saw another boat coming. As it got closer, he could see that it was a Game Wardens boat.

The Game Warden shouted. "You have some trouble? Need Help?" Slone stood up and said. "Yes, can you help me, please?" As the Game Warden got closer, he looked over in the boat. "Is he hurt? He said. Slone then looked over at him and said, "Yes, and I'm very sorry to have to do this." Slone then pulls his gun up and shoots the Game Warden in the shoulder, and he falls back into his boat.

He moves quickly and jumps into the Game Warden's much bigger boat. He finds the Game Warden alive, trying to get his gun out of his holster. Slone then quickly moves and takes the gun away from the hurt man. He also grabs the radio off his belt. He then rolls the man over on his back, opens the man's shirt, and looks at his wound. "Looks like the bullet went straight through. Where is your first aid kit?" The man just looked at him and didn't say anything. Slone then looked down at the man. "Look, I'm not going to kill you. But I don't have a lot of time here. Where is the first aid kit?" The man looked up at Slone and said.

"It's up under the passenger seat up front. Slone then went up to the front of the boat and got the kit. Keeping an eye on the man as he did. When he got back, he took some gauze and placed it inside the bullet wound. He taped a bandage over it. He took the man's left hand and placed it over it. "You need to keep the pressure on this."

He then went to the back of the boat, took his bolt cutter, and cut the battery cable. He took the bullets out of the man's gun and threw them and the radio overboard. He went up front and cut the mic off the boat's radio. He saw an ice chest, opened it, and found bottled water. He grabbed two bottles.

He then returned to the Game Warden. "OK, I have disabled your radio and motor. I found your water. Somebody should find you soon." He put the bottles of water down where the man could reach them.

He then went to the back of the boat and found that Cox's boat and the boat he stole had drifted away from the Game Warden's boat. He dove into the water and swam back to the boat he had stolen. Climbing in, he got loose from Cox's boat. He was going to dump Cox's body in the water, but that was useless now.

He started the motor and headed back to the part of the lake where he had left the van. When he got close, he killed the motor, dove in the water, swam to the bank, and made his way back to the van. He opened the back of the van and opened a box where he kept his stuff in. He took out one of the burner cell phones he had. He made a 911 call. When the dispatcher answered, he said. "A Game Warden has been hurt and is in his boat on Lake Limestone. He is going to need some help." He then threw the phone in the lake, got in the van, and drove back to the motel.

When he got back to his room, he quickly changed clothes and packed everything up. He put the 9mm and the silencer that went with it in a bag. They had gotten wet and would have to be cleaned before he could use them again. He took out his 38 pistol and put it in the holster under his left arm. He put a jacket on to cover it. He grabbed his bags, went down to the lobby, and checked out.

He put his stuff in the van and headed out of town. He would stay in Waco for a few days and see what happened. The game warden would be able to I.D. him now. But that could not be helped. He was just doing his job. Killing him would have been collateral damage. He didn't believe in that.

Waco was about 35 miles west of Groesbeck. On his way there he passed through the small town of Mart. As he was driving through town, a police car pulled in behind him and turned on his lights. "Oh shit," Slone said to himself.

He quickly pulled onto a side street so not as many people would see them and stopped. He puts the silencer on his 38 as he watches the cop in the mirror. The cop got out quickly. He had not had time to run the plates first. So, he would still be thinking it was just a minor traffic stop. But he would run them and his license and be on to him. He had to act now!

He jumped out of the car quickly. The cop shouted. "Get back in your car, sir!" Slone stopped and said. "I'm sorry." He pulled his gun out from behind his back and fired two shots at the cop, hitting him in the chest. He fell back on his back. Slone walked back to him. The cop was trying to get his gun out of his holster. He knelt down and took the cop's hand off his gun and took it out and put it out of the cop's reach. He rolled the cop over, took his handcuff out, and cuffed him behind his back. The cop was still gasping for breath. Slone looked at him and said as he picked him up on his feet. And said. "Calm down. Take slow, deep breaths. Your vest stopped the bullet. You're going to be sore and maybe have a broken rib. But you're not hurt badly." He then put the cop in the back seat of his squad car. The doors can only be opened from the outside.

He then returned to the van, got in, and took off. This day just couldn't get any worse!

*

John Carter had woken up early this Sunday morning. He had missed a rare chance to sleep late. Quietly showering and got dressed in a nice pair of starched jeans, a light blue shirt and his best pair of boots. He walked out of the bedroom to the kitchen and got a cup of coffee that he had started brewing before he got in the shower. His timing was perfect as the last few drops dripped from the coffee maker. He got a coffee cup out of the cabinet that had the S shield on it. With the words Super Dad under it. He always smiled when he saw it. It was a Father's Day gift from the kids.

After pouring his coffee, he put on his sports coat on and walked out on the back porch. He sat down at the table. He loved the peace and quiet. Just sitting here watching the sun come up.

After enjoying the sunrise, he got up and walked to the storage shed in his backyard. He opened the door and went inside. He came out with a small bag of sunflower seeds. He walked over to the picnic table, poured the seeds out on the table, and then returned to his chair on the porch.

He waited and watched. He didn't have to wait long. He saw him coming out of the corner of his eye. He jumped up on the picnic table and started eating the sunflower seeds. John smiled as he watched the squirrel he had named Rocky step back at him as he ate. Rocky was born in the trees around his house and had lived here all his life. John enjoyed watching him, and Rocky enjoyed the sunflower seeds he had been putting out for him for years.

A few minutes later, he heard the back door open and saw his son Tom come out on the porch. "Hey Dad," Tom said. Carter turned his head to Tom and said. "Morning, Tom." Tom looks out in the yard and smiles. "You feeding Rocky again? Ya know Mom says you spoil that squirrel." Carter stands up, takes the last drink of coffee, looks at Tom, and says. "Well, she spoils you." as he turns and opens the door. "They ready to go? Carter asks, and they walk through the door. "Yes," Tom says. "You know that you can spoil me too if you want. I'm like, ok with tha.t"

They walk through the house and join Carolyn and Becky. "Y'all ready to go?" he asks. Carolyn looks at him and says, "We are waiting on you." He grabs his Silverbelly cowboy hat from the hat rack next to the door and says, "Well, let's go."

They all get into the car and make the short drive to their church. Parking in the parking lot, they got out. Carolyn and the kids started walking toward the church, stopping along the way to talk to several people. Carter popped the trunk and walked to the back of the car. He removed the gun from his holster under his sports coat and placed it in the trunk of the car. He always wore his gun. Even when he was off duty. But I just didn't feel right taking it into the house of God. He then caught up with Carolyn and the kids, and they went inside.

He found his brother, Brian. He was a few years younger than John. He was also the Pastor of the church. They shook hands. Brian smiled. "How's it going, John?" Carter shakes his head. "I have had better weeks." "Ya, I have heard," Brian said. "You have any leads?" Carter looks down and then back at his brother. "No, not really. But we're working on it." At that time, the praise and worship team will be getting ready to start. People are moving to their seats. Brian pats John on the shoulder. "Get with me after service. I want to hear about it. I'm praying for you, big brother." Carter smiles. "I know. I need all the prayers I can get."

John starts moving toward where Carolyn and the kids are sitting. He and Brian had been close growing up, but they had taken very different paths. He liked to think that they were both good at what they did. They always supported each other. Many a time, he had to draw strength from Brian's words. He needed that more than ever now.

About 45 minutes into the service, Brian stopped abruptly and looked at the door as he picked back up where he had left off. Carter looked back to see what he had looked at. He was surprised to see Deputy Greg Roberts walking down the center aisle with his hat in his hand. He walked all the way down the 2nd pew, where Carter was sitting at the end. He bent down and whispered in Carter's ear. "We have another murder." Carter turns to his wife, who was already looking at him, and says. "I have to go." He gets up and joins Roberts, and they walk back down the long center aisle. As they walked, he could feel every head turn and every eye on them as they walked out of the church.

Outside, Roberts turns to Carter and says, "I'm sorry, John. When I called you and it went straight to voicemail I knew you had to be here. But I knew you would want to know." Carter turned and started walking toward his car. "It's ok. What do we got?" Carter stops at his car and pops the trunk. Roberts then says. "Well, the dead man is Stanley Cox of Mexia. He was killed in his boat on Lake Limestone. But get this. The Game Warden, Jeff Fisk, came upon them. He shot him too, but he is still alive." Carter had a surprised look on his face. "So we got a witness? How bad is he hurt?" "Not sure," Roberts said. Carter then puts his bible in the trunk, picks up his gun, and puts it in his holster under his sports coat. He then takes his wallet badge out of his back pocket. He flipped it around with the badge facing out and placed it on the pocket of his coat. This is how he wore it when he was on duty but out of uniform. He closed the trunk, and they walked over. Carter got into the passenger side of the patrol car that Roberts had come in. "Where did they take the Game Warden?" Carter asks. "They were on their way to the hospital here in town," Roberts said. Carter looked over at Roberts and said. "Let's go over there first and find out what we can from him. Right now he is our best shot we got at catching this son of a bitch!"

Carter and Roberts made the short drive over to the hospital. They entered through the ER and walked up to the desk, and Carter asked. "I'm Sheriff Carter. What can you tell me about Game Warden Fisk?

He was brought in here with a gunshot wound?" She looked up at him and said. The doctors are working on him now. He is in bay 4." "Thank you," Carter said as they walked down to bay 4. The curtain was pulled around it. So they waited. A minute later, a Doctor walked out. Carter stopped him and asked. "How is he?" The doctor looked at Carter and said. He was really lucky. The bullet passed right through his shoulder. They got the blood stopped quickly. He should be fine." "Great," Carter said. "Can we see him?" "yes sure." The doctor said.

Carter and Roberts opened the curtain and found Fisk lying on his bed with his shoulder bandaged. Carter walked up to the bed and said. "Mr. Fisk. I'm Sheriff Carter, and this is Deputy Roberts. If you feel up to it. We really need to talk to you about the man that shot you." "Ya sure," Fisk said. Carter pulled up a chair and sat down. Roberts pulled out his tape recorder and turned it on. Carter then said. "Ok, start at the beginning and tell us what happened."

Fisk then took a drink of water and then looked at the two men and said. "I was doing my morning lake patrol. I saw two boats together. I thought they might be having some kind of problems. I could see one man standing up in one of the boats. I asked if they needed some help. The man said yes. So I got my boat closer. About that time, I saw a 2nd man lying down in the boat. I ask. Is he sick? The man said yes. I pulled up beside them. That's when I saw the blood. I looked at the man standing there, and he said, I'm sorry, and he shot me. I fell down in my boat and tried to get my gun out. But the man jumped into my boat and took it. I thought then. He is going to kill me. But instead, he asks where the first aid kit is? He gets it and treats my wound. Tells me to keep my hand on it. He disabled my motor but left my trolling motor. So I can go for help. He then jumped out of my boat. I don't know where he went from there."

"OK," Carter said. "Do you remember what he looked like?" "Oh yes," Fisk said. "you don't forget the face of somebody that shoots you. He was tall, white, with dark hair, mustache, and goatee." Carter looks at him and asks. You think you could give a description to a sketch artist?" "Sure, I would be glad to try." He said. Carter takes a card out of his shirt and hands it to him. "If you can think of anything else. Please call me." Fisk nodded his head, and Cater and Roberts got up and left the room.

When they get outside, they stop and look at each other. Roberts says. "Ok, this guy goes to the trouble of stealing back his own DNA. Then he leaves a witness alive? Not only that. He treats his wound! What's this guy's deal?" Carter then starts walking toward the car and says. "He avoids collateral damage. He only kills his targets. He also could have killed the guard in the morgue. We are looking for a man with a lot of military training. Very disciplined and very, very dangerous!

Chapter 8

Jake Slone had made the short drive from Mart to Waco. Things had gone from bad to worse. After the Cox hit. He had to shoot a Game Warden to keep from getting caught. Then, to make matters worse. He was stopped by a Mart cop. Who he also had to shoot. He didn't think the Game Warden or the Cop were hurt bad. But they had seen his face. They would at least have a good description of what he looked like. Oh well, he couldn't worry about that now.

He drove downtown Waco, found a parking lot, and parked the van. He hated to do it, but he had to get rid of the van. The Mart Police would have the plates and a description of it. The plates were stolen so they would not lead back to him, but they would be looking for it now.

He locked the van, walked down the street to the bus stop, and waited for the bus. He took the bus down the street to a place with several used car lots. Getting off the bus, he looked around the car lot and found an older red Ford Ranger that would meet his needs. He went inside, talked to the salesman, and paid the man 3800 dollars cash for the truck. The man looked at him kind of funny when he counted out 3800 dollars in 100 dollar bills. But he took the money and didn't ask any questions.

Slone then drove the truck down the street to a hardware store and bought two large bags. He then drove the truck back to the parking lot where he had left the van. He got in the back and packed up all his stuff. Guns, knives, ropes, and all the stuff he had been using and might still need, and packed it up in the bags.

He then drove around until he found a rundown, beat-up motel. He checked in and went to his room. Inside, he looked around. This place was a real dump compared to the ones he had been staying in, but it would serve its purpose.

He sat on the bed, took out his burner cell phone, and called the man he was working for. When the man answered the phone, Slone said. "The 4th name has been taken care of." The man said. "Good! I will send your payment. Move on to the next name." Slone then said. "There have been some problems. I'm going to have to stop for a while." The man on the phone then said. "You have gone too far to quit now," Slone said. "It's getting too hot in town! I'm not going any farther!" There was a long pause on the phone before the man said. "I have taken steps to make sure you finish the job." "Like what?" Slone asks. "Your mother lives in Tulsa, Oklahoma, with a little girl. Your little girl. She is being watched 24 hours a day, and I have their phone taped. So don't try to call them. Just take my money and finish the job, and all will be great." The man then hung up the phone.

Slone sat down on the bed and stared at the phone. How was he going to continue? He wanted to quit and go to Mexico for a while, but he couldn't do that now. He had to keep his Mother and Michelle safe, and the only way to do that right now was to continue the contract.

*

Carter and Roberts had spent most of the day out at Lake Limestone. The dead man was a man named Stanley Cox of Mexia. He had been shot in the head just like James Johnson and Sam Logan.

They found one witness who saw a man swimming back to the bank, fully dressed, getting in a white van, and driving off. The Game Warden's description was the best break they had so far.

About that time, Carter's cell phone rang. It was Deputy Billy Hayes. Carter put the phone to his ear and said. "Hey, Billy." Hayes said on the other end. "Sheriff. I just heard that there was a shooting in Mart. A cop was shot by a guy matching the Game Warden's description. Driving a white van with stolen plates." "Ok," Carter said. That would go with the white van that was seen out at the lake. How bad is the cop hurt?" "Not to bad. He took two shots to his vest." Hayes said. "Good," Carter said. "We are going to need to talk to him. Call the Mart PD and talk to Chief Jack Garrett. Tell him what's going on and that I'm on my way." "Ok, will do," Hayes said.

Carter hangs up his phone, looks at Roberts, and says, " I guess we are headed to Mart."

Carter and Roberts make the 45-minute drive from Lake Limestone to Mart, Texas. They pull into the Mart Police station and go inside. Police Chief Jack Garrett sees them come in and walks over to them. He shakes hands with both Carter and Roberts and says. "Hey, John, your deputy called and said you were coming." They turned and walked into Garrett's office. Garrett sits down behind his desk, and Carter and Roberts sit in the two chairs facing the desk.

"Can I get you anything? Coffee? Garrett asks. "No, we are good," Carter says. "How's your officer that was shot this morning?" Carter asks. "He is going to be fine. He took two shots right to the chest. Thank God he was wearing a bulletproof vest. He is bruised up good. Do you think this is the same guy that's been doing all the killing up your way?" Carter looks over at Garrett and says, "Yes, I do." Garrett smiles back at Carter. "Well, this may be your lucky day." He opens up a folder on his desk, takes out a picture, and hands it to Carter. "Our dashcam got this picture of the guy getting out of his van." The picture showed a tall white man with dark hair and a goatee. Garrett then hands Carter another photo. "I had this one blown up." It showed the man's face. A little bit fuzzy, but his face nevertheless. Carter looks back at Garrett and says. "Thanks, this will be a big help." Carter then looks over at Roberts. "We are going to catch this son of a bitch!"

*

Slone got up early the next morning. He took a shower, shaved, got dressed, and went out. He walked across the street and bought a newspaper. He then walked down the street to a small café to get some breakfast.

Walking inside, the waitress smiled at him and said. "Good morning. Will you be dining alone?" Slone smiled back at her and said. "Yes, I will thank you."

They walked together down to a booth in the corner. He took a seat where he could see out the window and the door. It was a habit he had gotten into. She handed him a menu. He briefly looked over it and ordered: "Scrambled eggs, toast, and bacon with milk and coffee." She smiled and said, "We will get right on it." "Thank you, " he said.

While he was waiting for his food, he took out the newspaper and opened it. To his shock, he saw a fuzzy picture on the front page. It was him! He looked at what it said under the picture. It said this man is wanted in connection with the shooting of a Mart Policeman. He is also a suspect in the murder of Limestone County District Attorney James Johnson.

Holy shit! Slone thought. He had to get back to the motel and figure out what he was going to do. He called his waitress over. He said. "Something has come up, and I have to leave." He hands her a 10 dollar bill. "This should cover the meal." He then hands her a 20 dollar bill. "This is for you. I'm very sorry to be such trouble." She looks at him and says. "Thank you, sir. Let me get it put in a to-go box for you." He smiles at her and says. "Thank you. But I really don't have time."

He quickly walked out of the café and down the street back to the motel. Back up inside his room, he took out the paper and looked at it better. The picture was taken by the dashcam of the Mart Police officer. He had not thought about the Mart Police having that. Why did he get out of the van and walk back to the cop's car? The picture was a little fuzzy. But it was him! He had to think about what to do and fast! He wanted to run. He could be in Mexico before dark. But he didn't want to put his mother and his little girl in danger.

Ok, don't panic. Work the problem. He walked over, picked up his bag, and took out some clippers and gray hair dye. He went into the bathroom and started cutting the hair off the top of his head. When he got it as short as he could with the clippers, he took out a razor and shaved the top of his head to look like he was bald on top. He took out the gray hair dye and dyed the hair left on his head gray. He shaved his goatee off but left the mustache and dyed it also. He then put some brown eye contacts to cover his blue eyes.

He looked in the mirror. He looked 20 years older and not much like the man in the newspaper.

Chapter 9

John Carter finished his breakfast, put on his coat and hat, and headed to the office. He got in his car and drove to a gas station. He got gas and a newspaper. When he got back in the car, he looked at the paper. He saw the fuzzy picture of the man he had been looking for. He hoped the picture would lead to someone seeing him.

The one thing that bothered him was why? Why had this man killed these people? He didn't think any of the murder victims knew each other.

When he got to the office, he took out the box that had James Johnson's cases he had worked on and looked at them again. Most of his cases had been worked on by his assistants. He had only personally worked on one large case. It was the case of Mike McKinney. Johnson had got a conviction on McKinney for selling a huge amount of drugs. It was the largest drug bust in Limestone County history.

His father, Doyle McKinney, is a very rich man in Groesbeck. He got his son the best lawyer money could buy. But his son had been in trouble before, and the DA had a very good case. His father could not get him off this time. It was his third felony conviction. McKinney got sentenced to twenty-five years in prison. His father had been very upset with Johnson for going after his boy.

About that time, Deputy's Greg Roberts and Billy Hayes walked in. Carter looked up and said. "Sit down, and let's review what we got on this nut." Roberts then takes out a folder, looks in it, and says. "The 9mm gun used to kill Johnson was the same as the 9mm used to kill Cox and Logan. The van seen out at Lake Limestone matches the van stopped by the Mart Police. But the Mart police officer was shot with a 38 pistol.

Johnson, Cox, and Logan were all killed with a gunshot wound to the head. We also got O positive blood from the Pam Smith Murder. But can't say for sure it's the same man."

Carter looks up at them and says. "Ok, good. I also got a call from the Waco Police, and they found the white van in a parking lot in downtown." "Did they find anything in it?" Hayes asks. "No, it had been cleaned out. He knew it had been seen. So he abandoned it." Carter said.

Roberts looks up at Carter and says. "The thing that bothers me the most is why? What motive does this sick fucker have?" Carter then says. "That been bothering me too. I don't think he has been picking his victims random." Hayes got up and walked over to Carter's desk and said. "Why would he drive out to where Johnson and Logan lived, out in the middle of nowhere, and then go after Cox that lived in town? And probably Smith, who also lived in town?

Carter then looked at both men and said, "I think the answers might be in James Johnson's case files, specifically the Mike McKinney file. I want the two of you to go over it with a fine-toothed comb." If there is a connection, I want to find it!

*

Jake Slone got up later than usual. It had been the first night in days that he had been able to sleep. He took a quick shower and got dressed.

He saw the envelope on the table and picked it up. He had been avoiding looking at it for days, but he had to get started again. He took out the paper with the names on it. The first four names had been marked off. He looked at the fifth name. It was Mary Anderson. She was a middle-aged woman who lived alone.

He grabbed his keys and walked down to the parking lot. He got in the truck and drove to Mexia, where Anderson lived. He parked two blocks away and got out. His disguise made him look like an old man, so he took out a cane to walk with. He would look like an old man out for a walk.

When he got to Anderson's house, he looked at it carefully. It was a nice-sized house with a garage in the back. He saw Mary Anderson come home and park her car in the garage.

It was then that Slone decided to go forward with the hit tonight. He drove back to the motel in Waco and packed his bags and checked out.

He drove back to Mexia, found a cheap motel, got a room, and waited for nightfall.

At about 10 p.m., he drove back to the Anderson house. He parked down the street and walked back to the house. The lights were still on, so he waited.

At about 11:15, all the lights were turned off. Slone waited another 45 minutes for her to get to sleep.

He then walked over to the fence and jumped over it into the backyard. He walked over to the sliding door, took out his tools, and picked the lock. Inside the house, he took out his small flashlight. He walked through the living room to a hallway that must lead to the bedroom. He walked down the hall quickly to the bedroom in the back.

Inside, Mary Anderson was sleeping in the middle of the bed. He turned off his flashlight and walked over to the bed. He reached into his pocket and pulled out a rag that had been dipped in chloroform. He put it over her mouth. She woke up and struggled briefly before succumbing to the chloroform. He picked her up, carried her to the garage, and put her in the car. He went back and got a blanket and stuffed it under the garage door. He found a water hose, cut a long piece off, stuffed it in the car's tailpipe, and duck taped it around it. He put the other end of the hose into the car through a cracked window. He duck-taped the hole at the top of the window. He returned to the house, found her keys, came back out, and started the car.

He then waited for the carbon monoxide to come out of the tailpipe through the water hose into the car. He then went back into the house and out the back door, locking it on his way out. He walked back to the truck, got in, and drove around for a while.

He came back to her house several hours later. He walked up to the garage door and could still hear the car running. He got back in the truck, drove to a truck stop, and ate.

After eating, he drove back to the motel, laid down, and slept for a few hours. He woke up at about 7 am. He took out his cell phone and called the number. A man answered the phone. Slone said. "Number 5 has been taken care of, you son of a bitch!" The man then said. "Good, I thought you would see it my way! Move on to the next name." The man then hung up the phone.

*

Amy Barnes pulled up in front of Mary Anderson's house and honked the horn. She then picked up her newspaper and looked at it while she waited for Mary. She had known Mary for a long time. They had worked together at the Mexia State School for the last five years. About a year ago, they started riding to work together. One week, Mary would drive, and the next, Amy would drive.

She had gotten to Mary's a little early this morning, but after about 10 minutes, Amy went to the door to hurry Mary up. She knocked on the door and got no answer. She then rang the doorbell. Still, no answer. She looked in the window. It was still dark in the house.

Maybe Mary had forgotten it was Amy's week to drive and was at her house waiting on her. She decided to see if Mary's car was in the garage. She walked around to the back of the house. When she got to the garage, she could hear a car running inside. She beat on the garage door and tried to pull it up. But it was locked from the inside. She ran to the side door, which was also locked.

She ran back around to the front door, which was also locked. Amy now felt something was very wrong. She returned to her car, got her phone, and called the Mexia Police. She sat in her car and waited for the police to arrive. When they arrived, they knocked on the door and got no answer. She told them. "Go around to the back. I could hear a car running in the garage!" When they got to the back, they could hear the car running. They all tried to get in through the back. The police then ran around to the front and forced the front door open. She followed them through the house to the garage. When they opened the door to the garage, it was filled with carbon monoxide. The cop told her to call for an ambulance. She ran back into the house and found a phone and called.

The cop got Mary out of the car, carried her into the house, and started C.P.R. on her. But it was clear once the Ambulance got there that she was dead.

Amy was very upset. The cop said it looked like a suicide. But Amy didn't believe that. Mary was a very happy person. She would never kill herself.

Chapter 10

Slone got up at about 8 am. It had been about 24 hours since the Anderson hit. It had not been on the news. That was good. The police were looking at it as a suicide.

Slone went down and ate breakfast at the motel. Not the best breakfast he had eaten. But it kept him out of sight.

He walked out to his truck, got in, and slowly drove the 10 miles back to Groesbeck. He pulled up outside the Post Office. He parked his truck and got out. Remembering to use his cane and walk slower to look like a much older man. Several people were walking up and down the street. A man was selling watermelon and other fruit out of the back of his truck. He slowly made his way up the steps and into the Post Office. There were not too many people inside. He walked over to his box and opened it up. He reached in and took out the large envelope. He put it into his coat pocket and slowly walked back outside to the truck. After he got in, he took out the envelope and opened it up. All the money was there. There was also a smaller envelope inside. He opened it up and took out a small photograph. It was a picture of his mother's house and his daughter playing outside in the front yard.

The son of a bitch was telling the truth! He did know where his mother lived. He became very angry while he drove back to the motel. When he got inside, he walked over to the table and picked up the piece of paper with the names on it. The 6th name on the list was a man named Tim Baker. He was 45 years old, lived about 2 miles east of Groesbeck, and worked in an office building in Waco.

The next morning, Slone got up early, drove to where Baker lived, and waited. Baker came out about 7:30, got in his car, and drove to his job in Waco. Slone followed him there. He could have made the hit in the man's home. That would have been easier. But doing it in Waco meant a different County and a different Police Department. It might take them a little longer to connect the dots.

When they got there, Baker parked in front of a large office building. He got out and walked inside. Slone followed him in. Inside, there was a big lobby with a waiting area with couches and chairs, a TV, and restrooms. There were elevators on each side going up to the floors that housed several different businesses.

Baker got on an elevator and went up. Slone didn't follow him. He knew just how this hit was going to go now. He looked around some more and then left.

Slone returned at about 11:45 AM, sat on the couch, looked at a newspaper, and waited. At about 11:55 AM, Baker came out of the elevator and went into the restroom. Slone followed him in. Baker had taken the last stall. Slone waited for him to get seated. Slone took the stall next to Baker and closed the door. He took out the 9mm and put the silencer on it. He then stood on top of the toilet and looked down over the top of Baker's stall. He pointed the gun and fired a single shot into the top of Baker's head. Killing him instantly. Baker fell back still on the toilet.

Slone then got down from his toilet and opened his door. He went over to the urinal and used it. He washed his hands then went out of the restroom and left the building.

Slone then drove to a local steak house and ate a good meal before driving back to Mexia. On the way back, he made his phone call and told the man that number 6 had been taken care of. He then drove back to the motel.

He was going to have to pick up the pace. The police and sheriff were going to start putting it together. So he had to work faster.

*

At about 12:55 PM, one of Tim Baker's co-workers entered the restroom and used the urinal. As he washed his hands, he saw something red running out from under the last stall. At first, he thought it was some spilled soda. He walked down closer. He could now see it was not soda. He looked under the stall and saw a man's feet and saw what looked like blood around them. He beat on the door and shouted. "Hey, you ok in there?" When he got no answer. He forced the door open and was shocked by what he saw. Tim Baker shot in the head. There was blood everywhere. He ran and called the Police.

When Police got there, they sealed off the restroom. Detective Mark Lane walked into the restroom and saw Sergeant Hill and asked. "What you got, Sergeant?" Hill walks over to Lane and says. "Well, detective, we got a man named Tim Baker. A single gunshot wound to the head." Lane then looked at the body. "Anybody see or hear anything?" Lane asks. "No," Hill said. Lane then walked back out into the restroom area. "You would think in an office this big with this many people. Somebody would have heard a gunshot!" Lane said. Sergeant Hill looked over at Lane. "Yes, you would think so." Lane then walked and looked out the bathroom door. "Nobody saw anything?" Lane asks. Hill looked at his notes. "The only thing that was kind of out of place was an old man that walked with a cane. Nobody had seen him around here before." "Well," Lane said. "It's unlikely that an old man with a cane could have stood on a toilet and shot a man. But it's a place to start. Let's look at the cameras in the lobby and see if we can see what this man looks like."

Hill and Lane walk back out in the lobby and over to the main desk. Lane asks the man sitting behind the desk, "Where can we find the DVR for the cameras in the lobby?" The man stands up and says, "Right this way." The three men walk down the hall, and the man takes out a key and opens the door. "Thank you," Lane says as he and Hill enter the room and sit down.

Lane backs up the disk to about 11:45 a.m. They see the old man with a cane walking in the door. He is careful to look away when he gets close to a camera and sets with his back to it. When they see Baker come down the hall and go into the restroom, the old man gets up and follows him in there, and a few minutes later, he comes back out and leaves.

Lane looks over at Hill. "Looks like the old man is our guy. But he knows how to avoid the camera. I don't think we will have a single shot of his face.

Hill looks up from the TV. "He just walks in there, kills him, and walks out!" Lane stands up and says. "Ya, that's how it looks to me, too. Guess it's not even safe to take a shit anymore!"

*

Deputies Billy Hayes and Greg Roberts walked into Sheriff John Carter's office and sat down. Carter looked up and said. "What have you got?" Roberts said. "We were looking through James Johnson's case files, and I think we may have found something. The Mike McKinney drug case that Johnson prosecuted. It seems that Sam Logan, Pam Smith, and Stanley Cox were all on the jury." Hayes looked up and added. "McKinney's father, Doyle McKinney, is one of the richest men in the county. He helped Johnson get elected District Attorney. Then, Johnson prosecuted his son Mike and sent him to prison.

Carter then said. Ok, Billy. Greg and I will go see Doyle McKinney. You try to find the other jurors an eye on them."

Roberts then brought the car to the front, picked up Carter, and drove out to the McKinney place. When they got there, they pulled up in front of a huge house and got out.

Roberts looked over at Carter and said. "You could get lost in a big house like this." They walked up to the front door and rang the bell. A moment later, a woman answered the door. Carter then said. "Good Morning. I'm Sheriff John Carter, and this is Deputy Roberts. We need to talk to Mr. McKinney." "Come in, please," she said. She leads them down a long hall and into a large room. She smiled and said. "If you wait right here, I will tell Mr. McKinney you are here." "Thank you," Carter said.

In a few minutes, Doyle McKinney walked through the door and said. "Hello." As he shakes Carter's hand and asks. "What can I do for you, sheriff?" Carter looks at him and says. "We just have a few questions. Have you talked to your son Mike lately? McKinney then looked at Carter and said. " No. Not directly. I have sent and gotten a few letters." Carter then said. "Did you know that James Johnson was killed?" Yes, I read about it." McKinney said. Sam Logan. Pam Smith and Stanley Cox have also been killed." Carter said. McKinney frowned back at Carter and said. "Ok, what does that have to do with me?" " They were all on your son's jury," Carter said. McKinney looked Carter straight in the eye. If you check, you will find that Mike is still in prison and will be for a very long time. McKinney then took a card out of his wallet and said. "This is the name of my lawyer. Any other questions will have to come through him. Good day, Sheriff. He then turned and walked out.

Roberts then looked at Carter and asked. "What do you think?" Carter looked back at him and said. I don't know for sure. But I have a lot more questions for Mr. McKinney!"

*

Slone drove to the house of the man with the seventh name on the list. He sat outside and watched. He knew the local Sheriff Department had to be putting it together by now, so he needed to move down the list faster. It was the only way he could get this job finished.

The man's name was Fred Freeman. He lived in the small town of Kosse, about 15 miles south of Groesbeck. Slone had used his old man with a cane look to walk by the house and get a good look. He slowly walked back to the truck and waited for it to get dark.

At dark, he took a small bag out of the truck and walked back to the house and around to the back were Freeman's car was kept.

He lay down and got under the car. He reached into the bag and took out some plastic explosives, which he placed on the gas tank of the car. He then placed a remote control device in the explosives. He got out from under the car and took a last look around. It all looked good. He walked back to the truck, drove back to his motel, and got some sleep.

He woke early the next morning and drove back to Kosse to Freeman's house. The car was still in the driveway. He waited for Freeman to come out. At about 6:45 A.M., Freeman came out and got in the car. Slone then took out the remote control and waited for Freeman to start the car. When he did. Slone pushed the button on the remote. The car exploded, killing Freeman instantly.

Slone then started the truck and slowly drove by the Freeman house and watched the car burn.

Chapter 11

Carter and Roberts got back to the office about noon. They walked into Carter's office to find Deputy Hayes waiting for them. Hayes stood up and faced them and said. "I was looking for the rest of the jurors, and this is what I found. Mary Anderson was found dead in her garage from carbon monoxide poisoning, an apparent suicide. Tim Baker shot in the head at work in Waco yesterday. Fred Freeman killed this morning by a car bomb in Kosse."

Carter looks at Hayes with a shocked look on his face. "Oh my god," Carter said. "That means 6 of the 12 jurors are dead," Hayes said. "Ok," Carter said. "We got to get somebody watching the other 6." "I'm already working on that. We have deputies working on tracking them down now."

Roberts and Hayes then turn and leave the office. Carter sits down at his desk. When his secretary, Nancy Hall, walks in. She looks at Carter and says. "Mayor Boseman is here to see you." Carter frowns, puts his head in his hands, and shakes his head, then looks back up at he,r smiling down at him. He smiles back and says. "Send him in." She turns and walks out. A few moments later, Mayor Bobby Bozeman walks into Carter's office and says. "Good afternoon, John." He reaches over the desk to shake Carter's hand. Carter takes his hand and says. "What can I do for you, Mayor?" Bozeman takes a seat across from Carter and says. "My poll numbers are down. I feel like the reason is this rash of unsolved murders! People are scared. They need somebody to blame. So they blame everybody in leadership positions. I'm sure if you checked, you would find that your poll numbers are down too." Carter then looks at Bozeman and says. "The last thing I'm worried about right now is poll numbers!" Bozeman then smiles and says. "I had a feeling you might say that, so I have come up with a solution to our problem. Carter was sure he didn't want to hear this. But he said. "And what would that be?" Bozeman looks back at Carter and says. "You make an arrest. You find some low life scum bag and arrest him. We have a press conference. I put my arm around you and thank you. You thank me. We both get reelected, and everybody's happy. Carter then looks back at Bozeman with shock in his eyes. Not believing what he just heard. After a long pause. Carter says. "Everybody is happy! Everybody but the innocent man you sent to prison for killing seven people that he didn't kill! And how are you going to explain if the killings don't stop?" Bozeman holds his hands up to Carter. "I got this all worked out John. When the real killer hears that somebody has been arrested, he will simply let him take the blame and move on. And as for the scum bag that you arrest. He gets free room and board for a few months till after the election. Then, we quietly drop the charges and let him go with a small settlement. It's a win-win for everybody, John."

Carter sits back in his chair and says. "On top of being illegal and immoral, that's just so wrong on so many levels." Carter then points to the badge on his chest. It goes against everything this badge stands for!"

Bozeman stands up and says. "I was hoping you would see it my way. I'm going to have to distance myself from you. Worry all you want about what that badge stands for. But there may be another man standing behind it soon! Good day, Sheriff."

*

Groesbeck Goat head football coach Chris Young was getting his team ready for the biggest game of the year, against the Mexia Blackcats. The winner win's district.

The Sheriff Department had called and told him that they thought his life was in danger, something about a jury he had served several years ago. They did not want him to come to the game, but his players needed him. It was a big game for him, too. He had waited five years to win the district. This might be his last chance. The pressure to win was on all coaches, even in high school.

As his team took the field for warm-up. He felt silly with the two cops on each side of him. Plus the bulky bulletproof vest that they had insisted he wear. But he had to keep his focus on the game and his players. It was a big night for everybody.

*

Carter had just completed his third trip around the football field, looking for anything out of place. He had seen nothing. The stands were starting to fill up, and the players were coming out onto the field to warm up.

He had tried to talk Coach Young into not coming out on the field, but he wanted to be with his players, so he had to make sure all his bases were covered. He had Groesbeck Police in the stands on the Groesbeck side and Mexia Police in the stands on the Mexia side. He had his Deputies on the field with the players and coaches and in the parking lot.

He stood at the fence looking out at the field when Groesbeck Police Chief Joe Jordan walked up. "What do you think, Joe?" Carter said. Jordan stopped at the fence with Carter and said. "I think we got it covered."

Carter then looked over at Jordan and said. "Has the Mayor said anything to you?" Jordan smiled and said. "If you're talking about his plan to arrest some stooge and blame him for the murders till after the election. Then yes, I have talked to him." Carter smiled and said. "What did you tell him?" "Same thing that I'm assuming that you told him. That he is crazy. Then the little fat fucker asks me to resign. I said I wouldn't. So he is calling for a special city council meeting to vote on firing me." Carter turned and looked at Jordan with a shocked look on his face and said. "No shit! There is no way he has the votes for that." Jordan looked around the field and said. "No, probably not. He is just grandstanding. I heard he is giving a press conference tomorrow." "Oh, ya," Carter said. "He is probably going to unload on both of us. All the more reason to catch this sick fucker tonight!"

*

Slone put his bag in the truck and drove about a mile from the football field. He parked the truck, took out his bag, and walked to the water tower behind the football field. He put his bag over his shoulder, pulled the mask over his face, and started climbing to the top.

When he reached the top he looked around. He could see the whole city from here. It was over 200 feet tall and had a great view of the football field.

Slone then took his 308 rifle out of his bag and put it together. After he put the scope on, he looked through it to the football field to the Groesbeck bench. It would be a long shot, but one that he could make very easy. He then put the gun down, picked up his bag, took out a small parachute and put it on his back. He then went back to the rail and waited.

*

Carter walked up and down the fence just outside the field. He just knew something was going to go down here tonight. The game had started. The stands were packed on both sides. The Groesbeck Mexia game was always the biggest game of the year. He then heard a voice behind him. "Hey, Dad." He turned to find his son Tom standing behind him. Carter turned and looked at Tom with a surprised look on his face. "What are you doing here?" he said. Tom smiled at his dad. "I'm in high school now, Dad. This is a big game. Where else would I be?" Carter then looked around in the stands. "Is your sister here?" "Well ya," Tom said. "She is here someplace. Probably with her geek friends."

That was just great, Carter thought. Now, he had to worry about his own kids being here.

*

Slone waited for a clear shot. Looks like Sheriff Deputies were standing with him. They must be on to him. At the end of the first quarter, he had his shot, and he took it. Young was wearing a bulletproof vest. So he aimed at his head and squeezed the trigger of the 308 rifle. He watched at Young's head jerked back, and he fell to the ground. He then dropped the rifle and ran to the other end of the water tower. He climbed over the top rail and jumped. As he started to fall, he pulled the ripcord, and his parachute opened. The small chute opened, and he started floating down.

*

Carter heard the shot and grabbed Tom, forced him to the ground, and covered him with his body and drew his gun. Looking around, he could see Young lying on the ground in a pool of blood.

People in the stands were panicking, running all over the place. Police officers were looking around with their guns drawn. Carter then looked up and saw a parachute coming down from the water tower. He knew this had to be his man!

Carter got up off of Tom. Tom had a shocked look on his face as he saw his father with his gun drawn. He pulled Tom to his feet and said. "Find your sister and call your Mom to come to get you!" Tom shook his head. Carter then started running down the fence in front of the stands. Tom shouted after him. "Dad, be careful!"

Carter ran as fast as he could down the fence in front of the stands. As he came to the end of the stand, people were running in all directions. He could see the parachute getting close to the ground. Carter yelled at his deputies and cops, "The water tower!"

About that time, Carter heard a girl scream. "Help. Help me, please!" Carter looked up to see a young girl hanging over the side of the top of the stands. She must have been pushed over when everybody started running from the stands. Carter stopped and looked at the man's parachute fixing to land. He turned and started running back around and up into the stands. Quickly getting to the top. He reached over the side, grabbed the girl's wrist, and pulled her back up. When he got her back into the stands, she was crying. And grabbed him around the neck and held on tight. He put his arms around the crying girl, looked over her shoulder, and saw the parachute on the ground and a man running in the distance. He took a long look at the man. He thought to himself. You better run you son of a bitch!

By the time Carter got there, all that was left was a parachute on the ground. He told the cops and deputies that followed him to start looking around. He told Roberts to climb to the top of the tower.

Thirty minutes later he knew that the killer had gotten away again. Roberts had found a 308 rifle on the catwalk at the top of the tower. But he was betting that they wouldn't find any prints on it.

Carter, Roberts, and Hayes stood at the bottom of the tower. A Mexia Cop walks up and says. Is a Water tower even tall enough to parachute off of? "Carter and Roberts turn and both take a hard look at the cop. Carter then says in a raised voice. "Obviously, you can!"

Chapter 12

Carter got up early the next morning. He couldn't sleep. He hadn't slept well in for a good while now. He showered and shaved, walked to the window in the front door, and looked out. Reporters were camped out on his front lawn. A news truck was parked in front of the house.

They had been waiting for him when he got home. What could he tell them? Besides that, a killer had outsmarted him, and a man was dead because of it!

He had sent his wife and kids to stay with his mother so they would not have to face the reporters. It was only going to get worse if the Mayor carried through with his threat to hold a press conference this morning. It looks like he will not have any problems finding someone to talk to.

He cooked breakfast and slowly ate. He filled his cup up a 2nd time with coffee. Parachuting off a water tower! The guy was either really smart or really crazy, or both!

He walked over to his laptop, opened it up, and searched for the minimum height for a base jump with a parachute. He looked at the screen. "Well, I'll be damn." He said. There had been a few base jumps from as little as 100 feet. However, 185 feet was given as the minimum safe level. That would make our 200-foot water tower a safe level.

As he drank the last of his coffee, he thought of the nine people dead. Some had been friends of his. He had let their families down badly. He had always wanted to be Sheriff like his Grandfather. He had let him down, too.

He knew there would be calls for him to resign. Maybe that's what he should do. But he was not a quitter. He would see this through and find this guy no matter how long it took. Then, if they still wanted him to resign, he would.

He could not wait any longer. He got up and put his coat and cowboy hat on. He opened the door and walked through the reporters as they shouted questions at him. All of the witch he answered no comment!

*

Slone got out of the shower and got dressed. He expected the police to arrest him anytime. He almost wished they would. He wanted this job over with. He walked over to the table and found the list. The next name was that of Charles Lewis. He was in his 50s and worked out at Fort Parker. The Fort was a restoration of a Fort built in the 1800s to protect the settlers from Indians.

Slone then gathered his money and put it in a bag. He was going to mail most of it home. If he got caught, he didn't want to lose the money.

He then got in the truck, drove by the post office, mailed the money home, and then went to Fort Parker. When he arrived, he looked around and saw Lewis working at the big front gate. After taking a very good look around, he drove back to the motel.

He pulled up a map of the Fort online, studied it, and compared it to what he had seen. Then, he put together everything he would need and put it into the truck.

*

When Carter got to his office, the latest report on the Young murder was on his desk. He sat down and started reading. A few minutes later, Deputy Roberts walked into his office and said, "The Mayor is on TV." "Great," Carter said as he shook his head. He then pointed to the TV mounted to the wall in the corner of his office. "Turn it on, " he said. Roberts walked over and turned it on.

They both watched as the image of Mayor Bobby Bozeman came on the screen. "Last night. We all watched in horror as football coach

Chris Young was gunned down on the field last night! This was the 8th murder of an area resident. And the killer got away again! I'm telling you now. This must stop! We need action and leadership. I have to ask Groesbeck Police Chief Joe Jordan to resin, to which he has refused. So I will call an emergency meeting of the City Council to vote for his removal.

We then have Sheriff John Carter, who has been the lead on this investigation from day one! What has he done? I will tell you what he had done. Nothing but follow around two-step behind his guy. As the people around this County are killed!

I don't have the power to remove Sheriff Carter. Only the voters can do that. But I will be a voice for the people of this town and county! Thank you."

Roberts looks over at Carter and says. "Wow, I don't believe he did that." "Oh, I can," Carter said. "Maybe it's time we called the FBI and got some help."

At about that time, Deputy Billy Hayes walks into the office. He looks at them and says. "I think we might have a break. We have a witness that said she saw a man running away from the water tower and get in an older red Ford Ranger pickup. We also got the first numbers of the plate 856. Also, a truck fitting that description was seen at a motel in Mexia." Carter stands up and says. "Ok, let's get over to that motel!"

*

When Slone got back to his motel, he packed up all his tools, guns, grenades, and other explosive devices, put them all in a bag, and returned to the truck.

He wanted this job over! The sooner, the better. He had to work fast now. The police were just one step behind him now. Somehow, they had known that Young was his target last night. If that was the case, there must be something connecting all his targets. The last few names would be very hard. So he had to work fast now. He got in the truck and headed back out to the Fort.

*

Carter, Hayes, and Roberts pulled up in front of the motel and went inside. Carter approached the front desk and asked to speak to the person in charge. A man came walking out of a side office and said. "I'm Jim Fallon. I am the manager. How can I help you?" Carter holds up the picture taken by the Mart Police dashcam and shows it to the man. "Have you seen this man?" Fallon looks at the picture and says. "No, I don't know him."

Carter puts the picture away and says, "There has been a red pickup seen in your parking lot with the first plate number 856. You know anything about that?" The man walks over and starts looking through his paperwork. He looks up and says, "Ok, here it is. A red pickup with the number 856 NW3 is for a man named J. Smith in room 18." Carter says to the man, "Get the key and let's go."

They walk around the corner to room 18. Carter, Roberts, and Hayes all pull their guns, and Carter knocks on the door and gets no answer. Carter then turns to Fallon and says. "Unlock the door." Fallon then says. I can not invade the privacy of a guest. Not without a warrant!" Carter then turns and takes a hard look at the man and says. "I don't have time for this shit!" He takes the key away from the man and unlocks the door.

They quickly enter the room and find nobody in the room. They all put their guns away and start looking around. There were some dirty clothes on the floor and some papers on the table. Carter started looking at the paper. He found a list of names the first eight names had been crossed off. Johnson, Logan, Smith, Cox, Anderson, Baker, Freeman, and Young. All the people that had been killed. Well, they for sure had the right guy. The next name on the list was Charles Lewis.

Carter looks around at Roberts. "This guy Lewis must be his next victim. Do we have anybody on him?" Roberts then says. "No, we have not been able to find Lewis. He has moved from his last address we had and quit the last job we knew of." Carter then starts looking at more of the papers on his desk and picks one up. "It says here he works out a Fort Parker. We better start looking out there!

*

A school bus from Wortham, Texas, pulled up outside Fort Parker. Inside were 23 8th-grade students and their teacher, Laura Key. Laura had taught 8th-grade history for the last three years at Wortham Middle School. She loved her job and her students. She liked to get them out of the classroom and to where the real history had taken place.

As the students filed off the bus. Laura said. "Ok, everybody over here for a minute." The students then started crowding around Miss Key. "Ok, ok," She said. "Back up. You're breathing my air!" The kids laughed and moved back a few steps. She then said. "Spread out and look around. Go put your hands on the wall and close your eyes and try to imagine the Indians screaming trying to get in and the settlers gunfire trying to hold them off and what it might have been like." She looked around at her students, who were just standing there looking at her. She then said. Go, Now. Good day." One of the girl students said. "Aw Miss Key. Don't make us do that." Laura looked at her and said. "Good day." She smiled as they all turned and walked toward the Fort walls. They were going to learn something today.

*

When Slone got back to the Fort, he went inside with the bag with all his stuff in it. He looked around. It looked like about twenty or so kids were here with a school group. That was not good. He didn't like dealing with kids, but he didn't have any choice. He had to get this over and done with.

Just as he was about to make his move on Lewis, he heard Police sirens. He quickly looked outside and saw the cars of Groesbeck Police and Mexia Police and the Sheriff's Department. He pulled his gun, fired two shots in the air, and yelled. "Ok, everybody on the ground face down now!" Some kids screamed as everybody fell to the ground. He ran and closed the big front gate and locked it from the inside. He then ran to the smaller back gate and closed and locked it.

He looked through a small gun hole in the wall and saw Police coming toward the Fort. He fired his gun twice to keep them back. The cops then fell back to their cars. Well back from the Fort.

Slone then told everybody to get up and move closer together. After they had moved, he had them sit on the ground, and he looked them over. It looks like he had 23 students, probably about 8th grade. 1 teacher. 1 bus driver, 2 other men, and Charles Lewis.

The Fort had cameras on all four corners pointed inside. He went around and turned them all to face the outside so he could see over all four walls at the same time. The Police and Sheriff's Department had set up around all four walls, but well back.

Slone then called to Lewis by name and told him to go in the office and turn the monitors around so he could see them from outside the office. A surprised Lewis and did as he was told.

Slone then looked over the scared kids and said. "Look, if everybody is quiet and does what they are told, nobody will get hurt." He then pulled up a chair and sat down where he could see the monitors. There was no movement outside. But he was sure that would change. Things had really gone to shit. It was a good thing he had a plan B. He just hoped he could make it work.

Chapter 13

When Carter got to the Fort, he saw the red truck he had been looking for. He then called for backup from the Mexia and Groesbeck Police.

When he had the Fort covered on all four sides, he tried to move his men closer. But his men were shot a,t so he pulled them back.

Carter talked to the Director of the Fort Debbie Cotton who had somehow escaped. "How many people are in the Fort?" Carter asks. "Three Staff, a teacher and bus driver, and 20 or so 8th graders from Wortham middle school. Carter looked away and thought. Oh shit, we got a killer in there with over 20 kids. "Is there a phone in there?" He asks. "Yes," Cotton said.

Carter handed her his cell phone and said. "Dial the number for me." She punched in the number and handed the phone back to Carter. He let the phone ring a long time before he got an answer. A man picked up the phone. Carter said. "This is Sheriff John Carter. Who am I talking to?" The man on the other end said. "My name is not important." Carter then asks. "Is anybody hurt inside?" "No." The man said. "And if you want to keep it that way. You will keep your men back." "Good," Carter said. "You must have a name? What can I call you?" "Jake." The man said. "Call me Jake." "Ok, Jake," Carter said. "Why don't you let the kids go?" "No," Jake said. "Not right now." "Ok," Carter said. "How about some food and water? I'm sure the kids are scared and hungry." There was a long pause, and then Jake said. "Ok, get some food and water in here. Pull a van up to the gate. The driver stays in the car. I will send somebody out to get it. When we are back inside, I will let 10 kids go." "Ok, great," Carter said. "I will make that happen and get back to you." The phone then went dead.

Carter turned and looked at Hayes and said. "Ok, that's a start. Go get some pizza and some bottled water. "Will do," Hayes says as he turns and walks off.

Roberts walks up to Carter and says. "I just talked to a woman that was here with her 11-year-old girl and baby. She says the girl went inside while the mother was getting her baby out of the car seat. That's when the gates closed. So we have an 11-year-old girl inside someplace." "That's just great," Carter said.

"Just keep everybody back. But keep their eyes open. I'm going to exchange food for 10 kids. We are going to need to get one of our prisoner transport vans out here to pick up the kids in." "Ok, I'm on it," Roberts said as he walked off.

Carter knew he had to think his next move carefully. He couldn't make a mistake, not with that many kids' lives at stake. He needed to know what was going on in there. But how? Who would he send out to get the food? Who did he have the most control over? Who would get the food and come back and not run? The teacher! She wouldn't do anything stupid with her kids still in there. That's who he would send out.

Carter turned and looked around. The first Deputy he saw was Deputy Randy Fox. He walked over to Fox and said, "I need you to contact Wortham Middle School and find out everything there is to know about that teacher in there, and I need it yesterday!" Fox nodded his head and said, " OK, I'll get it, boss."

About 45 minutes later Hayes showed back up with the pizza and bottled water. They loaded it up in the big transport van.

Deputy Fox walks up to Carter and says, " Okay, this is what I could find out about the teacher. Her name is Laura Key. She is 26 years old, 5 foot 8 inches tall, has short dark hair, and wears glasses. She is very well-liked by her coworkers and students." "Okay, good. Thank you, " Carter says.

Carter saw Roberts walk up. "I need one of those two-way earbud transmitters and some other kind of listening device." Roberts ran and got what he needed and came back. They walked over to the van. Carter took the bug listening device and stuck it to the bottom of one of the pizza boxes. He then took the top box and taped the earbud to the top of the box. He put a sticky note on the top of the box that said. Laura put this in your ear. Roberts looks at Carter. "You sure it's going to be her?" Carter closes the van door. "Yes, I'm sure."

Carter picked up the phone and called into the Fort. The man answered quickly. "Yes, Jake. I have got your food. We are going to drive it down to the front gate. You get the 10 kids ready to come out. "Ok. The driver doesn't get out." The man said.

Slone hung up the phone and walked over to where the hostages were sitting. He walked up to Laura Key. She stood up. He looked at her and said. "Food is on the way. I'm letting 10 kids go. You need to pick the 10 kids." She looks him right in the eye and says. "There are 13 girls You will let all 13 go!" He smiles at her. "That was not the deal." She turns and looks at the kids looking back at her. "Let's go, girls. All of you get over by the gate." The 13 girls get up and move over by the gate. She looks back at the man with the gun and says. "That's the new deal!"

Slone smiles. He is kind of impressed with the ballsy teacher. "Ok. Have it your way. But nobody likes a smartass! When the van gets here, you can go out and get the food and water. When your back inside, the kids can go."

Laura walks over and joins the girls by the gate. Slone watches through a gun hole in the wall till the van pulls up out front. He walks over to the gate and opens it up. Laura walks out the gate, walks around to the side door on the far side, and opens it up. She sees Pizza boxes, and on the top box, there is a note that says. Laura put this in your ear. She pulls the note off and finds the Earbud. She quickly figures out what it is. She puts it in her left ear. She hears a voice that says. "Laura.

This is Sheriff John Carter. Can you hear me?" "Yes," She says. "Good," Carter says. "Now grab the pizza boxes and get back in there before he gets suspicious." She picks up the pizza boxes and starts walking toward the gate. She takes it inside and comes back out to get the water. Carter says. "Ok, Laura. I need you to be my eyes and ears in there. Only talk if it is safe to do so. Is everybody ok inside?" "Yes," She says as she turns and walks back with the water. She puts it down, walks over, and sits down with the boys.

Slone then opens the gate and lets the 13 girls out. They walk around, get into the van, and drive off.

Carter says. "I counted 13 kids. I thought we were only getting 10?" Laura says. "I made a better deal than you did!" "Ok, great," Carter says. "There should be an 11-year-old girl in there. Do you see her?" "No," She says as she looks around, she sees the foot of a child under the desk in the office. "Wait. I see her. She is under the desk in the office." "Good," Carter says. "That's as good a place as any right now."

Slone walked back and looked at the TV monitors. He saw that the police had moved closer. He had to do something to get them back. On the top of the walls, there were two cannons. He walked up to them, looked at them closer, and found that they were real. There were cannonballs sitting next to them. The only thing missing was explosives, and he had brought some of that with him. He then loaded one of the cannons on the east wall.

He then called Carter. When Carter answered. Slone said. "Get your men back on the east side." Carter then said. "Sorry, but I can't do that." Slone then said. "Ok. Maybe this will change your mind!" Slone then lit the fuse and fired the cannon. It hit and exploded in front of the police cars.

Carter's men hit the ground as the cannonball exploded in front of their cars.

Carter then looked at Debbie Cotton and said. "What the hell was that?" "Looks like cannon fire," Cotton said. "Cannon Fire!" Carter said. You got real cannons in that place?" "Yes," Cotton said. "This is a real Fort." Carter then looked at Cotton and said. "You mean to tell me a 150-year-old Fort has real god damn cannon's in it and I got a killer inside with 10 kids" Cotton looks at him and says. The cannons are real. We dry fire them several times a year for shows. The cannonballs are real, but just for show. We don't use them. He must have brought the explosives himself because we don't have any that could do that. Carter looks at her and says. "Well, that's just fucking great!"

Chapter 14

Slone watched as the police cars on the east side moved back. "I thought you would see it my way," Slone thought to himself.

He had started letting the kids come up and get pizza and water a few at a time. He looked into one of the empty boxes and saw the transmitter. He picked it up and looked at it. "Nice try, Sheriff, " he said as he dropped it and stomped it with his boot.

Laura says in a low voice. "He found your transmitter." "It's ok," Carter says. "I put it there for him to find. That way, he won't be looking for yours."

The phone rings. Slone walks over and picks it up. "What the hell are you doing?" Carter asks. "Just making a point," Slone said. "Ok, you made your point," Carter said.

"Ok, here is the deal," Slone said. "I want a van with a full tank of gas. When that gets here, I will let the rest of the kids and the bus driver go. The rest of us are going to drive to Limestone County Airport. You're going to have a plane fueled and ready for me. I will let the rest go then." "Ok," Carter said. "I will need a little time to get a plane ready." "You have an hour," Slone said as he hung the phone up.

Slone then walked back to the TV monitors and watched the outside. He knew that Carter was going to double-cross him somehow. He would get to the airport, and the plane would not have any fuel, wouldn't start, or there would be something to keep him on the ground.

Laura says in a low voice. "What's going on, Sheriff?" You need to get my kids out of here!" "We are working on that," Carter says. "We should have the kids out in less than an hour." "Good." She says. "My kids are scared, and this nut job is firing cannons!" "I understand," Carter said. "Just hang tight. What is he doing?" Laura then looks around and says. "He is watching the camera's and he keeps pulling a piece of paper out of his pocket and looking at it. Then he walks to the back of the Fort and looks around." "Keep watching him," Carter said. "Let me know if he does anything strange." "Ok, Sheriff." She said. "But hurry up!"

About 45 minutes later. Roberts walks up to Carter and says. "We found a plane. Nobody really wanted to give one up. But I was convincing." "Good," Carter said. Now, what do we do to keep him from getting on it and taking off?" He said he would let everybody go when he got to the airport. But what do we do if we disable the plane and he takes one of the hostages with him?" Roberts turns and looks back at the Fort and says. "That would not be good." Carter then says. "I think we have to let him take off and try to track him. It will only hold so much fuel. He has got to land sometime. So get a tracker on the plane. I think it's our only choice."

Roberts turns and walks away, and Carter picks up the phone and calls the Fort. When the man answers the phone, Carter says. "Jake, we have your van and plane ready." "Good," Jake says. "Drive the van down and park it at the front gate. Send another car with it and pick the driver up and take him back. Then I will let the kids go. And Sheriff, don't try anything stupid. I will be watching." "Understood," Carter says as he hangs up the phone.

Carter then had Deputy Hayes drive the van down to the Fort, and Deputy Fox followed him in a Sheriff's Department SUV. When they got to the front gate, Hayes stopped, got out, and got into the SUV, and they drove back.

Slone was watching through a gun hole as they drove away. He then walked over to Laura and said. Get the kids over by the gate and get them ready to leave. Laura got up and told the 10 boys who were left. "Ok, guys. Time to go. Get over by the gate." 8 of the 10 boys got up and walked over to the gate. The other 2 boys walk over and stand by Laura. She looks at them. They are two of her favorite students.

They were named Paul and Perry. "What are you doing?" She asks. "Get over by the gate!" Perry looks over at her and says. "We are not leaving without you, Miss Key!" She looks at them with a surprised and shocked look on her face. She says. "Ok, yes, you are! Go! Right now!" They look at her for a long moment. She looks back. "Thank you. But go!" "But Miss Key," Paul said. She points to the gate. "Good day."

The boys reluctantly start walking toward the gate. She calls back at them. "Hey, guys. Your book report is due tomorrow. I expect to see both of yours on my desk." Both boys nod and say. "Yes, Miss Key." They turn and walk to the gate and join the other kids.

Slone opens the gate and lets the kids and the bus driver come out, get on their bus, and drive away. Slone then turns to the others left and says, "Ok. Get over here." Laura, Charles Lewis, and the two other men walk over to the gate.

"Ok, here is the deal," Slone said. He handed Charles Lewis a ski mask. "Put that on. He said. Lewis then pulled the mask over his face. He then pulls a gun out from behind his back, takes the bullets out, and hands it to Lewis. "Ok, now. You're all going to walk out, you're going to point this gun at them. You all get in the van and drive off very fast. Understood." The three men say. "Yes."

He opens the gate, and two men and Laura come out and move toward the van. Laura says. "He is not with us!" "What do you mean? He is not with you?" Carter asks. "Just that," Laura said. "He is not with us. He is still inside." "Ok, Laura, get in the van and get out of there," Carter says.

They get in the van and start to drive away when they hear an explosion. Laura turns and looks out the back window, seeing fire and smoke coming out from the Fort. She thinks of the 11-year-old girl still under the desk inside. She screams, "Stop! Stop the van." The driver slams on the breaks and stops. She jumps out of the van and starts running back toward the Fort.

Carter is confused about what just happened. He looks and sees Laura running back toward the Fort. "Laura! What are you doing?" "There is a kid still in there." She says as she enters the gate back into the Fort."

"Oh, shit," Carter says. He looks around and sees Roberts. "Have your men tighten up the parameter," Carter said. Ok, now he looked around. He saw the Sheriff's Department SUV sitting there. He had to do something quickly. He ran and jumped in the SUV and started driving toward the Fort. Didn't know for sure what he was going to do when he got there. But he would think of something.

Inside the Fort, Laura could hear the little girl crying. She ran toward where she had last seen her. She found her still under the desk and pulled her out. "We have to get out of here," Laura said to the scared girl.

At that time, the corner wall weakened by the explosion fell. It hit Laura and knocked her down. She tried to get up, but her legs were pinned. The little girl turned and looked at her. Laura looked up at her and said. "Go hurry and get out of here." The little girl turned and ran.

As Slone was about to make his escape, he heard voices. He looked back to see the little girl running through the front gate. He looked back and saw the teacher lying on the ground. What was she doing back in here?

He turned and ran back to where she was. She looked up and saw him just before she passed out. He tried to lift the wall off of her, but it was too heavy. He needed something for leverage. He ran and pushed over a fence post and came back to her.

About that time, there was a big crash at the front gate. Carter had hit the gate with the SUV hard, knocking the gate off its hinges and landing on top of the SUV. Carter got out with his gun drawn. As he came around the front of the SUV, he could see a man with what looked like a fence post. He yelled at the man to stop. The man stopped, and Carter walked closer. It's only then that Carter saw Laura pinned under the wall.

Carter moves quickly to her side and feels for a pulse while still keeping his gun pointed at the man. She was alive. He stands up. Slone says. "She is going to die unless we can get her out of here. So either shoot me or help me. What's it going to be, Sheriff?" Carter looks down at Laura and then back up at Slone. He then puts his gun away. Slone puts the fence post under the wall and lefts. Carter pulls Laura's Legs free.

Carter then reaches down and picks Laura up in his arms. He then turns to Slone. Their eyes meet. "Give it up," Carter says. There is no way out. I have you surrounded." Slone smiles back at Carter. "I think I will take my chances, Sheriff." Slone then turns and disappears into the smoke. Carter then turns and carries Laura out the front gate.

Chapter 15

Carter stood and watched the Fort fully up in flames now. The fire departments were on the scene now, but the old dry wood of the Fort was burning hot and fast. His men had not found anybody coming out. There was no way he could still be in there and alive.

Roberts walked up. The teacher wants to talk to you before they take her to the hospital. Carter turns and walks back toward the ambulance. She is lying on a gurney at the end of the ambulance. Two men are waiting to lift her inside. He walks up to her. She pulls the oxygen mask off her face. "Did you catch him?" She asks. "Not yet. But we will." She looks at him. "Thank you for getting me out of there." She hands him the earbud that had been in her ear. "I think this is yours." He smiles at her. "You're welcome, and keep it as a souvenir." She puts the oxygen mask back on, and they lift her in the ambulance.

Roberts walks up and says. "We were looking there the stuff we found in the motel room and found this." He holds up what looks like a map of the Fort. Roberts points to a part of the map. "Is that what I think it is?" Carter looks at it and looks up at Roberts and says. "Find Debbie Cotton and get her over here."

Roberts leaves and comes back with Debbie Cotton. Carter takes out the map and shows it to her. He points to the place on the map. "Ms. Cotton, what is this?" She looks at the map and says. "This map shows Parker's old escape tunnel. Mr. Parker built it to escape if the Fort was ever overtaken by Indians. It was never used. The day the Indians attacked, the front gate was left open. They never had a chance to use it." Carter gives her an angry look. So there is an escape tunnel, and you didn't say anything about it." She frowns and looks up at him. "There was a tunnel. I don't even know if it's still there. We covered up the hole years ago. Didn't want anybody to go down there. We didn't think it was safe. We don't even talk about it anymore. It's not on any of the maps that are sold here at the Fort." Carter turns to her and says. "Ok. Thank you, Ms. Cotton." She turns and walks away.

Carter and Roberts look at each other and back out at the burning Fort. "I got a bad feeling about this," Carter says.

*

It was about 11:30 pm when Doyle McKinney went upstairs to go to bed. He had been watching the news about the fire out at Fort Parker. He walked into his dark bedroom and turned on the lights.

That's when he saw the man sitting in his chair. The man looked at him and said. "I have been waiting for you." "What are you doing here?" McKinney said. "Just some unfinished business." The man said. He then pointed to the safe. "Open it up." He said. McKinney walked over to the safe. "So that's what this is about. You're going to rob me." McKinney said. "No." The man said. "I'm not a thief." I'm just taking what you owe me." McKinney opens the safe and says. "I've paid you all I owe you!" The man then counts out 30 thousand dollars and puts it in his bag and puts the rest back in the safe. "Just what is this for?" McKinney said. I've paid you all I owe you!" The man looks up and says. "I won't even kill you for free. The man then raises his gun and fires. Hitting McKinney in the chest. He fell to the floor, dead.

Slone then walks over to McKinney's body and picks up his cell phone. He looks in the contacts and finds the name of Sheriff John Carter. He hits the call button.

Carter hears his phone ring and looks to see who is calling. He is shocked to see it Doyle McKinney. "Hello," Carter says. A familiar voice comes on the other end. He knows it's not McKinney. "Hello, Sheriff." The man said. "What do you want, and why are you calling on Doyle McKinney's phone?" "Well, John. Mr. McKinney and I just finished up our business together. So you can go back to being a small-town Sheriff. It's over." "Oh no," Carter said. "It's a long way from over. I'm going to come after you." "Suit yourself, Sheriff. I will be looking forward to it!" The man said as the phone went dead.

Slone then put the money bag over his shoulder, climbed out the window, and was gone.

Authors note

Hope you enjoyed Murder in Limestone County
Look for John Carter to return in Murder on a Hitman's Trail
<u>trebor4145@gmail.com</u>

Other books by Robert D. Coleman

Murder: The John Carter Novels
   Murder and the Cold Case, Book 1
   Murder in Limestone County, Book 2
   Murder on a Hitman's Trail, Book 3
   Murder and Redemption, Book 4
   Murder in the Old West, Book 5
   Murder through a Killer's Eyes, Book 6
   Murder and a Psycho's Revenge, Book 7
   Murder and the Private Detective, Book 8
   Murder in the Shadows, Book 9
   Murder on the Brink of War, Book 10
   Murder and the Long Ride Home, Book 11

Jake Slone: The Man in the Shadows Novels
   Jake Slone: Vengeance is Mine

Don't miss out!

Visit the website below and you can sign up to receive emails whenever Robert D. Coleman publishes a new book. There's no charge and no obligation.

https://books2read.com/r/B-A-ARIGB-VFSAD

Connecting independent readers to independent writers.

www.ingramcontent.com/pod-product-compliance
Lightning Source LLC
Chambersburg PA
CBHW051243160726
47994CB00002B/1002